THE IN-LAWS

A psychological thriller with a nerve-shredding ending

James Caine

ISBN-13: 9798835781669
ISBN-10: B0B2LT7NDQ

Library of Congress Control Number: 2018675309
Printed in the United States of America

CHAPTER ONE

Martha Jameson looked one last time in Henry's room, satisfied that everything was perfect for her *son* to return to. He was finally coming home after such a long time. Everything had to be perfect when he visited.

Martha smiled. She missed him. He barely came to visit now that he was older. He has visited even less since *she* came into the picture.

Beside the bed on the nightstand was a picture of her. Chelsea. His *wife*. She had long blond hair, and large blue eyes. The picture was of her in a long-sleeved white shirt. She's only twenty-one and beaming with beauty. She's gorgeous and from what Henry says, her soul is even more beautiful. This only angered Martha more. She turned the frame face down.

Martha looked across the room at a different picture frame on the dresser. She picked it up and stared at it. Martha was in her thirties when the photo was taken, and Henry was much younger. Her hand was wrapped around his shoulder. They were both smiling.

Those were different times though. Things are *different* now.

She moved the picture frame and placed it on his nightstand, replacing his wife's photo. She picked up the other frame of Chelsea and moved it to the dresser.

"Martha!" She heard his raspy voice calling for her but did not answer. She was caught up thinking about how things *used* to be. "Martha! Where are you?"

"Henry's room!" she called out to her husband. Arthur

1

limped into the room. He grimaced in pain when he stood beside her. "Leg hurting again?" she asked.

"It's the moisture in this old home," Arthur said, sitting on Henry's bed. He made a sound of relief when he did. "Mornings are getting harder."

Martha scoffed. "I just made his bed; get off!"

He nodded and stood up, grimacing again. Arthur coughed into his flannel sleeve. 'What time are they coming?"

"Should be around supper."

Arthur cleared his throat. "Good. I need more time to get ready."

"Finish in the garden first," Martha said sternly. When she didn't hear Arthur respond, she turned to him with a cold glare. Her husband was staring off into the room. She snapped her finger at him. "Are you going to be *ready* for Henry? For— his wife? Don't mess this up."

Arthur cleared his throat and pushed his disheveled gray hair to the side. "I won't."

"We need to keep our stories straight, right?"

"Right, Martha. Of course." He wrinkled his nose and stared off into the room again to Martha's dismay.

Martha sighed. "What's her name? Do you even remember?"

Arthur cleared his throat. "Chelsea."

Martha wasn't impressed. "You're going to mess this up for us. I know it." Before her husband could respond, she barked another order. "*Go*. Finish your work in the yard. I'll clean the house some more and get a salad ready from the garden for them."

Arthur didn't react as he left the room. She watched her husband limp on his left leg as he went down the hall. Time had not been kind to him. He was only sixty-five, but his body was that of a seventy-five-year-old.

Martha went down the hallway and stared out the front window. How much longer could Arthur stay out here? She had lived off the grid forever. They had their own garden, septic system, and solar panels. There were repairs to complete, maintenance tasks to stay ahead of. Could Arthur handle this lifestyle much longer? When Henry came, she would talk to him more about it.

Martha noticed a pile of white fluff surrounded by green grass outside. It was hard for her to make the white blur out, but it appeared to be moving. She took out her glasses from her dress pocket to take a closer look.

"Damnit," she said. "Not again." She tightened her lower lip as she looked at the dying chicken on the grass. She made her way outside the cabin. The grass surrounding the bird was stained with blood and feathers. The chicken moved its wings slowly. Martha picked it up by its neck and put it out of its misery with a twist.

She followed the path towards the barn where Arthur was already shoveling topsoil into a patch of small plants.

He looked at Martha and wiped the sweat from his forehead. "Chicken tonight?" He laughed to himself.

Martha was not amused. She raised its body to his face, dangling it rigorously. "That wolf is back! Set up some traps when you're done here."

He nodded. "Sure." He dug his shovel into the wheelbarrow full of soil and sprinkled it over the small plants. "Tomatoes are going to come in nicely I think."

"That wolf is going to *ruin* everything," Martha said, ignoring his comment.

"I'm almost done here," he said. "I'll put out a few traps. It's been weeks since we saw it. It will move on again."

Martha looked down at the tomato plants. They were sprouting nicely as he said. Then she noticed a dirty finger sticking out from the ground beside a leafy plant. She shook her head as she saw several other fingers from the hand sprouting out from the soil.

"No wonder why the wolf is back," she barked, pointing at the fingers. She looked closely at one finger. An emerald ring was clearly visible on one of the blue-hued digits. Martha bent over and wrestled it off. She rubbed dirt off the band with her fingers, and spit. "You need to do a better job, Arthur," she said sternly. "Henry is coming with his wife. It needs to be perfect."

Arthur nodded, stuck his shovel in the wheelbarrow, and covered the hand with dirt until it was fully hidden.

Martha smiled thinly. If things are perfect, Henry will never want to leave again.

CHAPTER TWO

Chelsea looked out the passenger side window, taking in the woods and mountains surrounding them as Henry drove off the highway into a gas station.

"You still have half a tank," Chelsea said to her husband with a smile. "Aren't we getting close to your parents by now?" It had already been over a two-hour drive from their apartment in Calgary.

Henry smirked. "First rule: when you live out in the middle of nowhere, always gas up when you can because you may not be able to until it's too late. Learned that lesson the hard way a few times when I was younger."

Henry parked his pickup truck in front of the gasoline pump. He turned off the ignition and smirked at Chelsea again. "How about I pump, and you go inside and get a few snacks for the rest of our road trip. Grab a few of those junkie gas station brownies too, I love those. Maybe a few for my parents."

"I thought your parents lived off the land. What do they need gas bar junk brownies for?"

"They taste delicious, that's all that matters. Pretty please, sweetheart." He opened the driver side door and got out, grabbing the gas pump.

Chelsea got out of his truck and stretched her legs. She looked around at the lonely gas station on the empty road. They truly were in the middle of nowhere.

"How much longer until we get to your parents?" she asked.

Henry opened the gasket but sighed to himself as he put

the pump back on the hook. "I'm getting used to the city now. They don't have pay at the pump options out here. When you go inside, can you ask them for $30 on the pump as well?"

"Sure," she said.

"And: about another hour and a half or two," he answered her with a grin.

Chelsea turned to walk towards the gas bar, but Henry whistled at her. She turned and he raised his wallet. "You may need this," he said. Chelsea put out her hand, but he waved for her to get closer, smiling.

"Stop playing games with me, Henry," she said with a laugh. "My back hurts and I want junkie gas station gummy bears as much as you want brownies." He didn't answer but kept waving her over to him.

When she was close enough, he grabbed her and pushed her against the side of the truck. He kissed her softly and leaned against her body. She could feel how *excited* he was already.

"There's something about being in the middle of nowhere with you that makes me want to tear your clothes off." he said, biting his lip.

"Stop," Chelsea said shyly. "Let's gas up, *first*." She kissed him.

He stepped back and raised her left hand, kissing her wedding band. "As you wish. Don't make me wait too long. I'm hungry... for *brownies*."

Chelsea shoved him. "You're trouble." She leaned in and kissed him again. Butterflies fluttered in her stomach every time she kissed her handsome husband.

The honeymoon stage, some call it. They had only been married for a few months and could barely keep their hands off each other. Even though Henry was thirty-four, he took good care of his body, and was successful, charming and funny. Sometimes Chelsea didn't understand what he saw in her. She was almost the complete opposite.

"Need gas?" an older, stockier man called out to them from the gas bar entrance. He stared at them awkwardly. "You have to pay inside."

"Sorry!" Chelsea yelled back. "Be right there."

"Why are you apologizing?" Henry whispered, raising his wallet higher.

"Stop it," Chelsea said back. "Give me the wallet." She looked back and the man was still staring at them. "He's watching."

"So what?" Henry said with a laugh.

"*Please*... give me the wallet?"

Henry lowered his hand. "Fine, I'm done playing around."

Chelsea snatched it from his hand, and when she turned to walk to the store, Henry smacked her butt. Chelsea looked back at him with an irritated face. She hated public affection like that. It was what others thought about it that bothered her most. As soon as she saw Henry's face, though, she felt nothing but his love.

"For that," she said, "I'm buying some potato chips too!" She walked towards the store and the old man went back inside the gas bar behind the counter.

She was amazed at how rustic everything was at the station. She spotted a phone booth beside the building and chuckled to herself. She couldn't remember the last time she saw a functional phone booth. She thought about going inside the booth and calling Henry from it to mess with him but decided the old man at the gas station had been waiting long enough for his only customers of the day.

When she went inside, she greeted the man behind the till, but he didn't respond. She went into the chip aisle and grabbed a few bags. She took her time going through the rest of the junk food aisle and spotted some gummy bears. Above them were the infamous brownies Henry had been craving. She grabbed a few bags and brought everything to the counter.

"Can I have thirty worth of gas, please, as well?" she asked.

The old man punched keys on his register and looked at her. "Forty-five," he said with a nasty tone. It was if her shopping in his store, with no other customers, was bothersome to him.

His curtness bothered her more. How many customers had he had today, being in the middle of nowhere? He can't smile or greet his customers? Thank them for saving his business? Instead of that happening, she paid the bill and thanked *him*.

She thought about what Henry said about the trip being another two hours potentially. She glanced around the small gas bar, looking for a washroom.

"Anything else?" the man asked.

"Is there a washroom here?"

Instead of answering, he pointed at a sign. "The Outhouse is for paying customers only." Below the sign was a hook with a key on it.

"When you're done using it, lock the door," he said.

"Never mind," Chelsea said with a smile. "Thanks." She turned to leave and saw a billboard beside the exit door. Although the board was small, it was stacked with missing persons posters. Some were piled on top of each other.

Chelsea glanced at a few posters. It amazed her to think all the pictures of the people on this board were missing. Someone out there was looking for them and they couldn't be found. How many of them were alive? How many were only runaways who wanted to stay missing for their own reasons? She hoped for most of these people it was the latter.

She noticed a weathered poster tacked underneath two others. Caroline Sanders. She had been missing for over two years. Last seen hiking the Grassi Lakes Trail in Kananaskis Country. At the bottom of the page was a case number and phone number to call with any information.

Chelsea took her time looking at the rest of the board at all the missing faces staring back at her. Most of them were older men and women, with a few exceptions.

"Do you want to buy some lottery tickets?" the old man asked.

"What?" Chelsea said.

The old man nodded at the lottery station below the

missing persons' board. "Just fill out your lucky numbers and maybe you could be the next one who wins. You saw that winning ticket on the board?"

Chelsea looked up at the board again. Below the posters of a few women was a picture of a lottery ticket. Handwritten, with poor lettering, were the words "$25,000 Winner."

"That could be you," the old man said with an ugly leer.

Chelsea was annoyed. The board of these missing people was desecrated with this man's greed. No wonder the missing stay vanished.

"I'm not that lucky," Chelsea said. She left the store without saying goodbye to the cashier. To her, that was the worst thing she could do to someone, leave without acknowledging them. To the old man, he could care less if he ever saw her again – or if her face was on the bulletin board some day.

"Excuse me, miss." Chelsea turned to see a young boy with pudgy cheeks on a red bicycle. Chelsea assumed he was around ten years old. His face was flushed red. Another boy who looked younger was sitting on a blue bike nearby.

"Yes?" Chelsea said with a smile.

"Well, I think we are a little lost," he said, lowering his head. "My mom told me not to go too far, but we didn't listen. Do you have a phone? Could I call her to come by and pick us up?"

"Of course." She took out her cell from her jean pocket and looked at the screen, noticing a new text from her friend Neil. She quickly read it.

"In-laws making you go crazy yet?" it read. Chelsea rolled her eyes.

She gave the phone to the boy on the bicycle. "Here you go."

The boy looked up at her. "The screen's locked though."

Chelsea waved her hand at him. "There isn't a password. Just swipe to open it. Do you want me to show you how to call someone?"

The boy put the phone in his pocket. He turned his bike

toward the road and jumped on the pedals. His friend on the blue bike was already starting to head off fast.

"Hey!" Chelsea yelled at the boy. "Stop!"

The boy on the red bicycle was laughing as he pedaled until Henry ran in front of him and knocked him off his bike. Henry quickly grabbed the boy and picked him up from the ground gently, but forcefully. Henry wiped dirt off the boy's clothes from the fall. He reached into the kid's pocket, grabbed the cell phone, and let go of the boy.

"Scram, kid," he said with a stern look. He watched as the boy picked up his bike and slowly started pedaling towards his friend on the road.

"Mike!" the boy yelled. "Wait for me!"

Henry looked back at Chelsea and slowly walked up to her; his hand stretched out with her phone. "I believe this is yours."

"I can't believe that happened," she said with a look of concern. "Those were, well, *bad boys*. Who does that?" She took her phone from his hand and opened it to make sure it wasn't broken. She was relieved when she saw it was fine.

Henry smiled. "When you move to Toronto, you better not be this gullible. That city will break you."

"Maybe we should call the cops?" Chelsea said, ignoring his comment.

"No, I lived in small towns my whole life. These boys are just *bored*. Thought you were an easy target."

"I'm not gullible!" she said. "The kid said he was lost. He needed my phone. I didn't want him to end up... on a missing persons poster."

Henry smirked. "*Gullible*," he repeated. He looked down at the junk food on the ground. He bent over and picked up a smooshed brownie. "Now, this is a *tragedy*."

Chelsea waved her head. "I'm not going back inside that gas station to get another one! That old man inside is the worst, and so are those kids."

Henry grabbed her hand and kissed her wedding band.

10

"Gullible and too sweet for your own good. If that old man was mean to you, you should tell him."

"He wasn't mean. He just... wasn't nice. I'm not that kind of girl to tell people what I think, you know that," Chelsea said, shoving him playfully. "That's why I married you."

CHAPTER THREE

Chelsea finished the last of her snacks as Henry pulled onto a dirt road off the highway.

"About another twenty minutes," he said, taking a sip of his warm cola. He turned his head to look at Chelsea and with one hand sternly on the wheel, he brushed his hand against the side of her face.

Chelsea welcomed his touch, even though she hated the gritty feel of his sandpaper fingers. For someone who was very successful, he had the hands of a man who worked physical labor every day of his life.

Before being a successful business owner, Henry did have a hard life. From what he was willing to tell her about him growing up, she knew it was difficult. His father built the cabin in Kananaskis Country, in the middle of nowhere, moving his whole life into the woods, dragging Henry with him. Henry was forced to drop out of high school and was taught at home by his mother. He had no prom, no best friends, only his parents.

It wasn't until he was old enough to demand more from his life that his parents let him leave. Henry said when he was seventeen and set out to live his own life, it was almost as if he went into a different world when he left the woods.

It was also difficult to find work without your high school diploma. He found stable work as a security guard and worked his way up to manager of the company within five years. Soon, an opportunity came to buy the company itself, and he took it. Now he owned and operated Secure Surveillance, one of the largest local security companies in the province.

Chelsea always admired that about him, his *drive*. He'd gone from being a jungle boy out in the woods to being head of the company and business owner of it all within a handful of years.

Chelsea was twenty-one, and still figuring out life. She was a struggling painter, trying to have her paintbrush make a mark. When her friend Neil said he was going to go to a prestigious arts program at the University of Toronto, and asked her to join, she knew this was her opportunity, and like Henry, she planned on taking it.

Henry didn't like it though.

The car started to slow as Henry rolled past a chain link fence. A large wood pole was cut in half, the other part face down in the grass below it. Soon they entered a wide, empty dirt parking lot.

Henry parked his truck. "We're here."

Chelsea smirked, waiting for him to say something that made sense. Instead, he turned off the ignition, and stepped out of the driver's seat. He stretched out his arms and moaned.

"What are you talking about, Henry?" Chelsea shouted. "We're in the middle of nowhere."

Henry walked to the back of the truck, lowering the bed and taking out Chelsea's backpack. "I told you, that's where they live, in the middle of nowhere." He pointed towards a grouping of trees. "We have to go about four hours that way." He looked back at Chelsea with a smile, but she didn't return it. "What?" he said. "I'm not messing with you, it is!"

Chelsea sighed. "What did I sign up for?"

"A whole weekend of *fun!*" Henry answered with enthusiasm.

"It feels like it took a whole weekend to get here."

"And just four more hours to go." Henry handed her her backpack and Chelsea wrapped it around her shoulders. Henry put his on, and shut his truck bed, locking his vehicle with his fob key.

They walked for an hour into the woods. Chelsea tried to

keep things lighthearted, but she was annoyed at Henry. Usually, when frustrated with someone, that person would never know that Chelsea felt hurt, but Henry was the only person to whom she was ever able to say what was on her mind. It was the reason she fell for him quickly. She felt safe with him. She could open up to him about her life, everything she had gone through.

She lost her mother at a young age, and during the past year, her father as well from a heart attack. Henry was with her the whole time. He saw and understood her emotions, sometimes better than she did.

"Are you going to tell me?" he asked. Henry ducked under a low-lying tree branch and looked back at her. As Chelsea reached the branch, he lifted it for her until she was through. "You're upset? Is it because I dragged you out in the middle of nowhere to meet my parents?"

"No," Chelsea said, lowering her head. "You don't really think *poorly* of me, do you?"

"What do you mean?"

"*Gullible*? I mean, you don't think I'm stupid, right?"

Henry stopped walking and grabbed her hand softly. "No, I don't. I think the world of you. Gullible was... the wrong word to use. You're... just a good person. Some people try to take advantage of that."

Chelsea nodded. "Those boys could have needed help."

"I take it when you left the store, you didn't see the one on the red bicycle slip his cell phone in his other pocket?"

Chelsea furrowed her eyebrows. She didn't. How many people have those boys tricked? she thought to herself. She remembered the missing people on the board in the gas bar. "Well, that doesn't matter," she said. "Maybe their cell died, and they needed help. Sometimes people need help, and need good people, like me."

"You're right. Maybe I think too negatively of people. I'm...sorry, okay?" He wrapped his hand around her waist and pulled Chelsea towards him, kissing her gently. "I mean it."

Chelsea smiled. "That's why I love you, Henry. You can

admit to things. Please, don't ever change."

Chelsea held his hand tight. She remembered something her father told her, in his last few months while in the hospital recovering from another heart attack. "That man is special, Sea," he told her. Sea was a nickname he'd had for her for as long as she could remember. Her father had told Chelsea that her eyes were like her mother's and were as blue as the Atlantic. Her father didn't say it, but she knew he wanted to see her get married. She was his only child. She had dreamed of him walking her down the aisle, but with his deteriorating health, knew it wouldn't happen.

One night, on a random date, Henry surprised her with a party at her favourite restaurant with friends and her father waiting. That night, he proposed.

She covered her mouth in shock when Henry got down on one knee. Although they had only been together for six months, she was already head over heels for him. After he asked for her hand in marriage, Chelsea quickly looked at her father, who nodded in agreement. Soon after, her father's health began deteriorating further. Chelsea and Henry initially planned to have their wedding at a church with a large party after, but none of that mattered to her anymore. Like every girl, Chelsea had dreamed about what her wedding day would be like, and she had big plans for it, but if her father wasn't there, it wouldn't have mattered.

Henry agreed to have the wedding within two months, and they were able to quickly get everything in order. Chelsea's father did walk her down the aisle. In the end she did have the wedding she wanted because the people she cared about most were with her.

Unfortunately, Henry's parents weren't able to attend. Chelsea hadn't even met her in-laws until this weekend. When Chelsea asked why they couldn't come, Henry rolled his eyes, telling her how particular they were. They hadn't left their cabin in the woods in years. Henry would bring anything they requested to them, if they needed anything, which was rare.

A month after the wedding, Chelsea's father passed.

Now it had been almost four months since he died. She grieved for her father but was starting to see the other side of her heartbreak.

Henry was with her the whole time, and she loved him even more for it. She felt bad for not being the newlywed wife he had dreamed of. Instead, she was a tearful mess. Now she was getting her life back on track, though. Now she wanted to go to art school in Toronto, and after, focus on her life with her husband, and maybe even a few kids along the way.

Chelsea got her foot stuck in some mud for a moment and twisted it out. She looked around at the dense woods surrounding them. How did Henry even know where to go? There was no discernable path. When she asked him, he said he knew these woods like the back of his hand. All she saw were trees and bushes, but they were like road signs to Henry.

"I thought you were used to camping as a kid?" he said.

"My father always took me," she said, "but nothing like this. We went to popular camps, and when he was older, we would rent RVs. Nothing off the grid, like you or your parents."

"Make sure to tell my parents that," he said. "The last girl I brought to them didn't know a lick about being out in the woods."

Chelsea laughed. "Here I was thinking I was the only girl you brought out in the middle of nowhere."

"Only a few I brought home to the parents," Henry said. He looked back at Chelsea and smiled. "They are going to love you."

Henry had said that a few times already on their trip. The more he said it, the more pressure she felt. What if they *hated* her?

She had assumed his parents were the type to not want to be around people, given their chosen lifestyle. She had asked to meet them several times, but only now was Henry able to make it happen.

"I'm happy I finally get to meet them," she answered.

"It's the perfect weekend for it, too," Henry said. "I've got a huge project starting soon. It's going to be super busy. You have art school potentially starting in a week. Before all these hectic things happen, we get to spend some quality time with my folks."

Chelsea felt bitter when he said "potentially" going to art school. She wasn't sure what he hated more, the idea of her leaving the province or her going to school with Neil. They had talked and argued about it many times over the past month. Henry felt she was rushing into something, but Chelsea knew she was ready to start her life again. Neil wasn't a sexual threat to Henry. Since the first time they kissed, Chelsea only had eyes for her husband. With his looks and charm, it wasn't too hard to maintain. Neil, on the other hand, was just *Neil:* nothing more than a good friend.

Chelsea thought about saying something but didn't want to argue about it.

"Are we almost there?" she asked.

Henry nodded. "About an hour or so left."

"Ugh. I have to pee!"

Henry looked around the woods. "Pick your potty."

"An hour?" she repeated. "Fine!"

"What?" Henry laughed. "When you were in the Beavers when you were younger, you didn't go pee outside?"

"Beavers was for little boys. *Girl Guides* were for girls," she corrected.

Chelsea found a large tree and went out of sight from Henry. She pulled down her jeans and panties, and cautiously looked around before releasing. She hovered over a pile of leaves and felt a flick of urine on the side of her legs, making her wince. A sound of crunching leaves getting closer made her almost jump.

"Henry!" she yelled. "Can a girl get some privacy around here?"

The crunching sound stopped.

From a distance, Henry began shouting, "Eh Bear! Go

17

Bear! Go!"

Chelsea froze. She heard movement from a bush near her, and the sound of something whizzing off into the woods.

Henry ran up to her. "Are you okay?"

"Was that a bear?" Chelsea managed to say between deep breaths.

"I'm not sure," Henry said. "It was something *big*. It's gone now."

"Oh boy!" Chelsea said, taking a deep breath.

"Didn't they teach you in Girl Guides that most of the animals out in the woods are more scared of you then you are of them?" He reached out his hand and Chelsea grabbed it. "Let's hurry up. We can get there soon."

It took Chelsea some time to shrug off what happened, but when she found her pace again, they got to their destination. They soon made it to an area free of bushes and trees. She spotted the roof of a wood barn.

"Oh, thank god," Chelsea exclaimed. Henry laughed.

A fence made with wood and nails surrounded a large clearing. They followed a dirt path that went to the gate. Henry lifted the latch to open it, and Chelsea noticed a large sign tacked to the fence that read "Do Not Trespass" and another below it that read "Property Under Video Surveillance."

They walked down the path that led to a large one-storey cabin. Chelsea's father would have loved a place like this. He would have enjoyed booking a vacation at a cabin in the woods. She couldn't imagine living here year-round, though.

"You should see the large garden in the back," Henry said. 'I'm sure my parents will show you. They're so proud of it."

Chelsea did enjoy gardening. She'd had a small tomato plant at their apartment in Calgary but somehow killed it within a few days.

Henry walked up the wood stairs to the front door, with Chelsea taking her time behind him. He knocked and waited.

Chelsea noticed a camera on the porch facing them. Henry answered her before she could ask.

"Runs on a generator," he said. "I installed their whole system. It's amazing what you can do now."

Chelsea nodded and waited anxiously for the door to open. She heard no movement from inside the home. She peeked inside a window and saw three fabric chairs sitting beside a metal fireplace. There were no lights on inside, or movement.

Henry knocked on the door again, harder. "Mom! Dad!" he yelled. After another minute of waiting, he looked at Chelsea. "I guess they're not home. Maybe we should go back to the truck and come back a different time?" When Chelsea didn't react to his joke, he laughed to himself. "They could be in the garden." Henry waved at Chelsea to follow him down the porch steps, but then she heard a creak at the front door.

It slowly opened, and a woman wearing a black dress to her knees stepped out. Henry had told Chelsea that his mother was in her early fifties but could easily have passed for a woman in her forties. Her thick, dark eyebrows raised when she saw Henry.

"Henry!" She wrapped her arms around him tight. "Please, come inside. Your father and I have been waiting all day!" She forcefully grabbed him and guided him inside.

Henry shouted, "Dad!"

Chelsea smiled to herself, taking in the moment of seeing Henry reunite with his family.

His mother noticed her. Immediately her face, once bright with happiness, slumped to a more neutral demeanour.

"You must be Chelsea," she said to her daughter-in-law. Before Chelsea could answer, Henry's mother turned from her and gestured for her to follow. "Come inside!" she yelled to Chelsea.

CHAPTER FOUR

Martha shut the door behind Chelsea and looked passed her towards her son.

Henry bear hugged his father. He beamed in a way Chelsea hadn't seen before. For a moment Henry almost seemed like a young boy when hugging him.

"I missed you," he said to his father, letting go. His father nodded. He turned to his mother. "Mom!" He gave her an even tighter squeeze, wrapping his hands around her waist. "I can't believe how long it's been."

His mother cupped her hand around his face and smiled. Chelsea could feel the warmth of love Henry had for his parents, and for a moment was struck with envy. She couldn't help but think of her father.

"You just need to visit us more, Henry," his mother said.

Henry pointed at Chelsea. "Mom, Dad, meet my wife, Chelsea."

His father gave her a thin smile. Martha's warm expression for her son quickly disappeared when she looked at Chelsea.

"You must be tired from traveling," his father said to them.

Chelsea nodded. "It took some time."

Arthur smiled wider. "I bet Henry didn't tell you about the four-hour hike to get to the cabin, did he?"

Chelsea smiled back. "No, he sure didn't, but I'm glad I finally get to meet you both."

"Us as well," Martha said. "Henry has told us so much

about you when he visits." She looked at her son. "Which—"

"Yes, yes I *know*, Mom," Henry said with a sigh. "We need to do more."

His mother raised an eyebrow. "Well, even without your pretty wife, Henry, you can visit us *anytime*."

Chelsea could feel tension from his mother's words. Was she suggesting Henry wasn't visiting so often because of her? Did they not know that even Chelsea at times had to fight for Henry's time and affection? Was this somehow Chelsea's fault?

"I'm excited to be here. Henry told me so much about your cabin and your lifestyle. I can't wait to experience it."

"Just wait until you see how you go to the washroom out here," Arthur said with a chuckle.

Martha struck him in the shoulder. "So *vulgar*, stop it. This is how we live."

Chelsea felt a sense of grief again. Had she managed to offend her mother-in-law again? "I didn't mean to insult your lifestyle, Mrs. Jameson. I meant that I'm interested in experiencing it while I visit. The first of many visits. I'd love to see your garden more too. My father had a small one in his backyard but nothing like this."

"Well," Martha said with a thin smile, "most people don't depend on their garden to live like us."

Henry wrapped his arm around Chelsea's shoulder. "Chelsea has some experience in the woods, but nothing like our family. We will have to show her the ropes."

Arthur took a pipe from one suit jacket pocket, and a bag filled with tobacco from the other. He opened the bag and put some in the pipe. "We can certainly show her. Should we start the *grand* tour?"

Martha looked at him sternly. "Dinner is almost ready, Arthur. The tour can wait until after." Arthur took a match out of his pocket, and lit it, nodding at his wife. "We're having chicken stew tonight."

"Can't wait, Mom," Henry said.

"Why don't you go to your bedroom and settle in," Martha

said.

"I guess the tour starts with my bedroom," he said. His father laughed but Martha maintained her grimace.

"Dinner will be ready in fifteen minutes."

For a moment, Chelsea felt like a teenaged girl and wondered if Martha would tell Henry that if he brought a girl into his bedroom that he needed to keep the door open.

Chelsea looked around the home, and the antique fabric chairs beside a large fireplace in the living room. The head of a wolf was above the mantle. The head of a buck and a few large fish decorated other parts of the walls. Although it wasn't how Chelsea would make a living room, there was an authenticity to the setting. The wood paneled walls made the larger cabin look smaller, almost cozy.

Henry grabbed her hand. "This way, hon."

Chelsea stopped and looked back at Martha. "You have a lovely home, Mrs. Jameson."

Martha glanced at Henry, then at her. "Why thank you."

Arthur stood beside his wife, blowing a puff of thick white smoke from his mouth. "And please, stop calling us by our last names. We're family now. Arthur and Martha would do from here on."

When they stood beside each other, it was much easier to see the contrast between the husband and wife. Arthur, visibly much older, looked frailer, weathered. His hands were wrinkled, but appeared strong for his age, gripping his pipe between his fingers. His disheveled grey hair was a shade above salt and pepper.

Martha was younger and had a slender physique. While she appeared smaller and weaker than Arthur, Chelsea could feel the power that radiated from her aura.

Henry grabbed Chelsea's hand and guided her down the hall. As they got further away from his parents, she could hear them talk to each other. It almost sounded like they were bickering. Arthur shushed his wife loudly.

Henry opened a door in the hallway and waved his hand

into the room. "I present to you: my *bedroom*." He smiled as Chelsea sauntered in.

Chelsea took her time looking inside. It was tidy and neat, just as Henry was. That was something that had always surprised her about him. Most men she knew hated cleaning and could barely take care of themselves, but not Henry.

His room was immaculate, as if it had been cleaned today. Meeting his mother, Chelsea knew Henry must have gotten this trait from her and wouldn't have been surprised if Martha did clean his room for him.

She noticed books on survivalism and horticulture on the bookshelf. The only thing out of place was a poster of a half-naked Pamela Anderson.

Henry noticed Chelsea staring at it. "I used to be a big fan of *Baywatch*. I should have taken it down years ago. Don't be jealous."

There was a photo of her on his dresser. It was a picture that Henry took on their first date. She remembered the exact moment he took it. After a full night of laughs and drinks, Henry took out his phone and asked if he could take a picture to remember the best date of his life. Chelsea thought the line was corny but loved his delivery of it and agreed.

"I'm also a big fan of her too," he said pointing at Chelsea's picture.

Chelsea smiled and sat on his bed. "Ugh," she said. "A bit harder than I thought it would be."

"Not too many Posturepedic mattresses can be delivered out here," Henry said.

Chelsea turned her head and noticed another picture frame on his nightstand of a much younger Henry with a woman's arm around him.

"Whoa!" she said out loud. "Did you leave a picture of you and your ex on your nightstand?" Chelsea laughed.

Henry's smirk faded. He grabbed the frame, looked at it for a moment, then outside into the hallway. Henry shook his head.

Chelsea put his hand on top of the frame, sliding her fingers across his. "I was just joking. I know you don't come here much. What was her name again? Your ex?

"Carrie," Henry said, "but this isn't her. It's me and Mom."

Chelsea grabbed the picture frame and stared at the picture again. Martha had her hand wrapped around Henry with a large smile on her face. Perhaps that's why Chelsea hadn't noticed it was her at first.

"She was beautiful when she was younger," Henry said.

"Your mom is still a good-looking older woman."

"She had me when she was fifteen," Henry said. Chelsea knew the story. Henry had told it to her many times. He truly adored his mother. He talked about how much she had to give up for Henry. She didn't finish high school. She had to raise a child while Arthur worked. The hardened woman Chelsea met at the front door didn't seem so scary when she looked at the photo.

"She hates me, doesn't she?" Chelsea said.

"My mother? No, of course not. She doesn't even know you yet. All my parents hear are the amazing stories I tell about you."

"I thought I'd have a harder time with your father. I thought it would be easier to get along with your mom."

"Mom is great once you get to know her. She's like a female lion, protecting her cub, even if that cub is in his thirties. You're a part of this family now. She will feel the same way about you soon enough too."

"From how you talked about your father, I thought he would be the stern one."

Henry lowered his head a moment and looked back at Chelsea. "My mom is… hard around the edges, but it's all mush in the middle once you know her."

From the moment Martha opened the front door, Chelsea had felt tension. It was as if her mother-in-law was able to communicate to her without saying it. *This is who my son married? She isn't good enough.*

Chelsea looked at Henry. "You said you brought other

24

girls to meet your parents here, right?"

"Yes, not many."

"Did your mom get along with them?" Chelsea asked, looking down at the picture frame again. "Did they like... Carrie?"

"They did." Henry grabbed the picture frame from Chelsea. He went across the room and placed the frame on the dresser, putting Chelsea's picture on his nightstand. He sat on the bed beside Chelsea and patted her leg.

"Do you know how much I love you?" he asked. Chelsea nodded. Henry smirked. "No... I need you to say it."

"A lot."

Henry leaned in and kissed her forehead. "You don't need to worry about anything. My parents, my mom, they are going to see how great you are. Do you know why?"

Chelsea looked at Henry's brown eyes and could feel the warmth of his love. "Why?" she asked.

"Because you're great. Amazing even. Anybody can see that, and they will too."

From down the hall, Martha shouted, "Dinner's ready."

Henry smiled at Chelsea. "Don't forget: it's only a weekend."

CHAPTER FIVE

Martha

As Henry guided his wife down the hallway, Arthur smirked at Martha.

"What?" she asked.

"She's nice," he said. Martha didn't respond. "Very pretty too," Arthur continued.

Martha bit her lip. She knew Arthur was trying to rile her up, and she wouldn't take the bait. Instead, she went to the oven and stirred the stew.

"She is a beautiful young *girl*," Martha managed.

"I said *she's nice*, Martha. You want Henry to stay here, you will have to be too."

"What do you know, *old man*?" she sneered back. "I know what I'm doing. Do you?'

She knew that would bother him.

Arthur shushed her. "Not so loud."

Martha looked down at the pot, taking in the scent of potatoes and other vegetables. The smell of the cooking meat made her mouth water.

"Like I said, old man, I know what I'm doing. I've done it before. You, on the other hand—"

"Stop." Arthur threw a hand in the air. "No more. They need to stay, and you are already making that hard."

Martha turned to look at her stew, stirring it slowly. She watched the bubbles in the pot pop, exploding sauce around it.

Henry needed to stay, but maybe there was a way for

his beautiful wife *not to*. She looked outside at her garden and smiled.

Arthur stood behind her. She could feel his presence, his anger at her. It made her smile wider.

"When are you going to tell him?' Arthur asked in a whisper.

"When the time is right," Martha answered, stirring the pot. She took out her spoon and banged it on the side of the pot. "Don't worry about that. Just stick to the story, if you can remember it." Martha looked at her husband. "Dinner's ready!" she shouted.

CHAPTER SIX

Chelsea sat at the table while Martha served bowls of stew in front of each of them. Chelsea had offered to help but Martha declined. The three of them sat in silence as Henry's mother took her time going to the kitchen and coming back with their meal.

Martha put a bowl in front of Arthur first who sat at the head of the table. He nodded at her in appreciation.

When Martha placed a bowl in front of Henry next, he breathed in the fumes from his stew. "Smells great. This makes the long hike all worth it."

Martha went back into the kitchen to grab another bowl and put the meal in front of an empty chair. She brought Chelsea's bowl last.

"Thanks, Martha," Chelsea said, but Martha didn't respond.

Martha sat at the other end of the table and smiled at her family. Chelsea smiled back and grabbed her spoon.

"Let us say grace," Martha said. Chelsea quickly lowered her spoon and hoped she hadn't noticed. She looked briefly at Henry, who had a smirk on his face. "Thank you, God, for Henry coming home, and for us being *whole* again." Martha paused a moment before continuing. "Thank you for bringing Chelsea into our home as well."

Arthur raised a glass. "Grace."

"Grace," Martha repeated.

Henry reached under the table and patted Chelsea's waist. "Grace," he whispered.

Chelsea lowered her head. "Thank you. *Grace*." When

everyone else grabbed their spoons and dug it into the yellow broth, Chelsea joined in.

They ate in silence for what seemed like forever to her. Finally, Arthur stirred up a conversation. "How's work, Henry?"

Henry nodded and swallowed what remained in his mouth. "Good, good. We got a big contract in the city. It's taking a lot of time, but this contract will easily be 35% of our revenue this year. We can hire a few more salespeople, installers. It's going to be a good year."

Arthur smiled. "You have done good work with your company. Proud."

Henry looked at him warmly. "Thanks, Dad. That means a lot."

"Soon Superior Surveillance will be the largest in the province," Arthur said, scooping a spoonful of stew.

Henry exchanged a glance with his mother and looked back at Arthur. "It's Secure Surveillance, Dad."

Arthur shrugged. "Yes, sorry."

"Hopefully we will get even bigger though," Henry said softly. He smiled at Chelsea. "Can you believe that even in some remote cabin I can install a security system?" He pointed at the panel above the door. "It lights up red when the system is armed."

"Why have a security system out here?"

Martha responded. "You never know what some of those crooks from the city will think of doing. When we lived in the city, we had *problems*, even a break-in when we were not home. They ruined our door."

"Don't forget about the wildlife," Arthur said. "Especially bears. Smart creatures. A while ago, a black bear managed to get inside the cabin." He laughed to himself. "Martha almost shit herself when she saw it in our kitchen."

Martha frowned. "*Language!*"

Arthur waved her off. "Henry scared it off with pots and pans."

Chelsea looked at her husband. "No way!"

Henry put down his spoon. "I don't like bragging, but I scare away bears. It's what I do. I'm basically a superhero."

Martha dug into her stew with her spoon. "Now he's not here so much, so I wanted a security system. All the windows are shatterproof glass too."

Chelsea looked at the large window in the living room.

"Go ahead, Chelsea," Arthur said. "Take that living room chair and throw it into the window." He laughed. "It won't break, I promise."

Chelsea looked at Henry. "How can you install a system out here, though?"

Henry pointed behind him at the cabin's wall. "Multiple generators outside. They power the home and the system. It's even wi-fi compatible, but with the cell tower being so far away we only get faint bars that aren't stable. Sometimes you can get cell reception inside. Usually, you'll have to go deep into the garden, though, to call someone."

"Henry," Arthur interrupted, "that reminds me, we're having trouble with that wolf again. Pretty sure it's the same one as last time."

Chelsea looked into her jean pocket and pulled out her cell phone. She saw another unread message from Neil. She put the cell back in her pocket and when she looked up, Martha was staring at her. Chelsea quickly turned away to Arthur.

"Can you help me with some traps later?" Arthur continued.

"Of course, Dad,' he replied.

"The wolf got one of our chickens, too, today," Martha said.

Chelsea glanced down at a piece of chicken on her spoon and back up at Martha, who smiled at her.

"I'll take care of it," Henry said. "After all, I can handle bears; I'm sure a wolf would be easy." He smirked at Chelsea.

Chelsea put her spoon down and cleared her throat.

"You, okay?" Henry asked.

Chelsea nodded as she grabbed her glass of water, taking

30

a sip.

"Do you not like my stew?" Martha asked.

Chelsea waved her hand. "No, it's lovely. I'm just... full, thank you."

Martha looked at Henry. "Your wife is a stick; she needs to eat."

Arthur laughed. "I'm not sure how you're wearing a long sleeve shirt like that too. It's boiling hot here." He picked up his napkin and waved it in his face. "The sun beats down on our roof, and with how the home is built, it basically absorbs heat."

"I'm okay," Chelsea said, pushing her white sleeve into the palm of her hand.

"Well, it cools off at night, sometimes, so maybe you'll be okay," Arthur said.

"So," Henry said, changing the subject, "you know that Chelsea is an *aspiring* painter, right? Did I tell you that she's going to the University of Toronto's art program?"

"No," Arthur said. "I hadn't heard that. Congratulations, Chelsea."

"Thanks."

"*Toronto*?" Martha repeated. "What about Henry?"

Chelsea moved around in her chair. "Well—"

"Mom," Henry interjected. "It's okay. She's going to come back between semesters. I'll visit her too."

"I couldn't imagine being away from my husband for *so* long," Martha said, lowering her head. "And all by myself? In such a terribly large city, riddled with criminals?"

"She's going with a friend," Henry said.

"Well," Martha continued, "even if she brought a friend, two girls can't fend off predators."

Chelsea breathed in deep. She could immediately imagine Henry telling his mother that it wasn't another woman but a man who was coming with her to Toronto. His mother would rip into her about how wrong that would be. A woman doesn't travel with a man beside her husband.

"Times are different now, Mom," Henry said. Thankfully

he kept Neil's name to himself. He really was a *superhero*.

"When do you leave?" Arthur asked.

"School starts the week after next, so I'm probably flying out soon," Chelsea replied.

"That's great," Arthur said. "Your parents must be proud too."

Chelsea lowered her head and looked back at Arthur. "They have passed... both of them are not with us."

Henry exchanged another glance with Martha.

Arthur lowered his spoon. "Of course, Chelsea, I meant—" He pointed to the ceiling. "From up there, you know?"

Martha stood up abruptly. "Well, who's ready for dessert?"

CHAPTER SEVEN

After everyone finished their dinner, Arthur insisted on starting the tour of their cabin.

He raised his hands around the living room. "We can start here," he said enthusiastically. "Sorry – we don't have too many guests these days, so it's nice to show off what we've done to this place. It's really something."

Chelsea looked around the room. Everywhere in the home had a wood smell to it. You somehow knew instantly that it had been built by Arthur, especially given his enthusiasm. "It really is beautiful," she said to him. She wondered how on earth could someone build a cabin like this in the middle of nowhere and felt she would save that question for later. It could be something she could ask when the conversation died down or if she felt stricken by an awkward silence with her in-laws.

Arthur pointed at the fireplace. "I tend to feed the fire most of the day and it keeps the whole home warm. Winter can get tricky, but we insulated the exterior walls and installed heat pumps to keep heat in and coldness out. That's why it's boiling hot here. I do hope you brought some lighter clothes, Chelsea."

She smiled politely but didn't respond. Chelsea looked at the head of a buck on the wall and pointed at it. "You must be a hunter?"

Arthur turned and looked at the animal. "Was a hunter, is more like it." He patted his left leg. "An old injury that didn't heal so well. I can't get around like I used to. I stick mostly with fishing these days, or trapping animals."

Henry stood beside Chelsea, grabbing her hand. "Dad," he

said, "get to the main event. The garden is your pride and joy, besides me."

Arthur smiled. "I do take pride in it, but Martha gives it all the love. Without her, everything out there would shrivel and die within weeks of me tending to it. I put in the work, and Martha makes it come to life."

Martha shook her head. "Here he goes again. Arthur, I put a lot of labor in there too, just like you."

"Yes, dear, you do." He limped towards the main door and waved for everyone to follow. "We're losing light outside, hurry now." Chelsea smiled when she noticed how bright it was outside.

The four of them went out the door and walked down a dirt path to the garden. Arthur started pointing around different areas. "Over there, you have the apple orchard." The area covered thirty feet or so. "Grapevines and raspberry bushes are over there." He pointed in another direction. "Spice and basically all types of fruit/vegetables are spread amongst the garden from here."

They continued down the path as Arthur explained what was growing in each area. Chelsea was definitely amazed at the work put into the garden.

"How do you guys find the time to do all of this?" she asked.

"We... don't get out much." Arthur laughed.

"We have enough to feed three or four mouths for a couple months off fruit and vegetables alone," Martha said. "Not to mention whatever Arthur catches or traps."

Chelsea nodded. "It really is something. My father loved to garden. He only had a planter box filled with small vegetables." She noticed a short stem emerging from the ground. She walked over to it. "This is a tomato plant, right? My father loved growing them in his little box. He would have loved your garden."

Martha frowned a moment at her, and Arthur gestured for her to come over to him. "Sorry," he said, "growing new plants there. Try not to step close to them if you can. Those babies need a lot of love and attention to grow right."

Chelsea looked around at the small plants, and the pile of loose soil near her foot. "So sorry!" She stood up and hurried back over to Henry, grabbing his hand.

"Not your fault," Arthur said. "We would put out signs, but nobody comes out here besides Henry." He started walking slowly down the path again. "Over this way is the barn."

Close to the garden stood the large, rotted out barn Chelsea spotted before. The wooden walls looked damaged and weathered. It appeared that a strong wind could blow it over at any moment. Chelsea wondered if she pushed with all her might if she could topple it.

When Arthur showed them inside, he pointed at the workbench and cabinets. Under the counter was a large tarp. He pointed at his fishing poles. On the other side of the barn on the ground were rusted traps of different sizes.

Arthur gestured at a big trap with large metal teeth. "Can you help me load that one, Henry?" Arthur looked at Chelsea. "They truly aren't hard to load, it's just moving them that's difficult for me."

Chelsea nodded. She looked at an old black and white photo tacked on to one of the cabinets. "Who are they?" she asked.

Henry answered. "My grandparents. They came from Ireland originally. They built their own homes back then too. See that small house in the back?" Chelsea squinted her eyes and looked at the home behind the young couple. "Well, they built that themselves. When my parents moved out here in the woods, they wanted to go back to their roots, just like my grandparents lived. Built this home themselves."

"I'm amazed at how beautiful your lifestyle is out here." She looked at Martha, who for a change smiled back at her.

How could they live out here year-round? The winters could be brutal. The wildlife was dangerous. She would never want to come out here if there was the potential for heavy snow.

They could be stuck inside the cabin for days. The thought of that made Chelsea cringe inwardly.

A chicken ran across the barn suddenly. "There must be another hole in the coop," Martha shouted. She looked at Arthur sternly. "We need to fix that if we don't want the wolf hanging around our property tonight."

Arthur rolled his eyes at Chelsea. "Like I said, I'm the labor; she gives the love."

Chelsea let out a laugh and when she noticed Martha's grimace, quickly shut her mouth.

Arthur pointed at one side of the barn. "The chicken coop is on the other side of the barn. I hope you're an early riser, because our rooster is." He laughed to himself. "Well, that's everything outside. There's a shed over there too. You basically saw the whole inside too already." He put a finger to his mouth. "Oh, wait. Follow me!" He walked towards the cabin. "I almost forgot."

Martha followed her husband, maintaining her sour face as she did. Henry grabbed Chelsea's hand.

"Unfortunately, I know what he wants to show you now," he said. "I'm sorry in advance for this weekend."

Chelsea laughed. "Don't be. Your dad is hilarious."

Martha looked back at her, then turned and continued following her husband.

When they were back inside the home, Arthur walked past the kitchen and living room.

"You've already seen Henry's room." He gestured at the open door. "This is the master bedroom," he said, pointing at the closed bedroom door beside Henry's. Arthur walked across the hallway and opened another closed door. "And the washroom."

Chelsea wrinkled her face in preparation at what she was about to smell but was pleasantly surprised at first. A porcelain sink was in front of her. On the other side was what looked like a white bench with two toilet lids on top with a large bucket beside it.

"I have to say, I was expecting worse," Chelsea said with a

smile. "You hyped it up too much, Arthur."

"Wait for it," Henry said.

"We use a bucket system," Arthur said. "We take turns emptying the bucket each day. Now that there's four of us, I will probably have to do it a few times daily, but we will take turns." Chelsea tried not to react. He pointed at the toilet lid on the left. "This one's for number one only," he said, and gestured at the other. "I'm sure you know what that one is for now. When it's time, take the buckets and bring them to the compost bin outside."

Chelsea was still focused on him alluding to her carrying their pee and poo buckets until she realized he said the word *compost* as well. Her face soured.

"Did you say *compost bin*?" Chelsea said in shock.

Arthur laughed. "That's what I was waiting for." He laughed again. "Well, Chelsea, you can't find good manure out in the middle of nowhere. Our soil needs good nutrients."

Chelsea felt lightheaded for a moment. She had dined on food filled with her in-laws- *nutrients.* She felt like she could puke but maintained her composure.

"It's not a big deal," Martha said. "Better than eating whatever pesticides are on the fruits and vegetables you buy at the market. That stuff causes *cancer*! It's not like we dump the bucket on the garden itself."

Chelsea took in a deep breath. She hadn't meant to upset her with her reaction. "I'm sorry, Mart—"

"Mom," Henry interjected. "She didn't say anything bad. This is all new to her, okay."

Martha nodded. "Well, it's nearly nighttime, and I'm sure you both must be exhausted."

"Maybe we can garden together tomorrow," Chelsea said. "I'd love to see how you manage it all."

"*Plenty* of time to show you," Martha said with a smile. "Goodnight, Henry." She leaned in and kissed her son's cheek.

Henry rubbed the saliva off the side of his face. "Miss you too, Mom. Goodnight."

"Goodnight." Chelsea waved. She thought about giving her in-laws a hug. The expression on Arthur's face was welcoming and she took a step closer to them.

"Goodnight," Martha responded. She walked across the hallway, took a key out of her dress pocket, and opened her bedroom door.

"It was a pleasure meeting you," Arthur said. "Goodnight." He followed his wife into the bedroom and shut the door behind them.

Chelsea went inside Henry's room and looked out the window and although the sun was beginning to set, there was still plenty of sunlight left. She had never visited someone where the hosts would abruptly leave for their bedrooms the way they had.

"And," Henry said with a smile, "those are my parents." He leaned in and kissed her. "Can you see why I like to bring everyone over?"

Chelsea put a finger to his lips. "Shh. I'm sure you can do everything in this cabin."

"My parents are early risers," he said. "I'm not surprised they go to bed at this time, just saddened." Henry closed his bedroom door.

"I thought maybe we would play board games, or something," Chelsea said.

"My parents? *Games*? I don't think so.' Henry patted the bed, and Chelsea sat beside him.

"What do they do for fun then out here?"

Henry laughed. "Work, cook, build stuff... argue. They are very good at that, as you can see."

"I'm sure all parents do that well," Chelsea said. She looked at the closed door. "Is your mom going to get upset that you have a girl inside your room with the door closed?" she mocked.

Henry laughed. "She likes to look out for me, too much, I know. She wouldn't ask me to do that with you – we're married."

"So, that other girl you brought here, Carrie something,

you were never able to close the door?"

"That's right," Henry said. "And that was only two years ago."

"Henry! You're thirty! I can't believe that."

Henry shrugged. "Their home; their rules."

"Well, now I feel special," she said with a smile.

Henry kissed her neck gently and rubbed the inside of her thigh. "So much left of the day," he said. "How could we *pass* the time?"

"Henry," she said in a whisper, "I can't. *I can't.*"

"What? Why *not?*"

"She's your mother, but do you have no clue..."

"What?" Henry said, waiting.

"I mean, she's *scary*... intimidating. I can't have sex with you *here*. I can't. *Stop.*" She grabbed his hand and threw it off her lap. "We can wait." Henry gawked at her. "Stop," Chelsea repeated. "You know I would, but the last thing I want is for her to walk in here."

"She won't," Henry said. He began kissing her neck again, the way she liked. She felt electricity run through her whole body. All it took was a few more kisses there for her to give in.

Chelsea let out a soft moan and closed her eyes in frustration. "Fine, but make it quick, and quiet." She stood up to lock the door, but to her horror found out the door couldn't. She looked back at Henry; her mouth gaped open. "You have no bedroom lock?" Henry smiled again. "Okay, *nope*. Sorry. *No way.*"

"Okay, okay, okay." He stared up at her from the mattress and patted beside him. "I promise I won't *bother* you."

Chelsea sat beside him. "It's only for a weekend, Henry," she said mockingly. She laughed and Henry smirked. Her smile vanished suddenly. "Okay, I couldn't ask this before, but did the stew your mom made, was it made with the chicken the wolf killed?"

Henry laughed. "What?"

"The chicken we ate at dinner. Your mom said a wolf killed a chicken today. Was that the one we ate?"

Henry thought for a moment and shook his head. "I know my parents are different, with their composting and stuff, but we wouldn't eat a half-eaten chicken. My parents aren't that *crazy*."

"Okay. I'm not sure why I thought—"

"Stop," he said. "Tomorrow, you and I will go hiking around the property, just us. Give us some alone time. I know my parents can be a lot, I do, and I appreciate that you're here."

Henry looked outside the window. Chelsea did the same and took in the beauty of the sun beginning to set over the tall trees.

"I need to tell you something," Henry said. "I wanted you to meet my parents of course, but there's another reason we had to come."

Chelsea waited a moment for him to say more, but he didn't continue. He stared outside the window; his lips moved but he couldn't find the words. Chelsea took her hand and slowly guided his head towards hers. She kissed him softly.

"What's wrong?" she asked. "You can tell me."

Henry kissed her lips again and lowered his head. "It's about my *father*."

CHAPTER EIGHT

Martha

Martha told Arthur to shut the door behind them as they stepped into their bedroom.

"A bit early for bed, no?" Arthur said, unamused, as he locked the door.

Martha ignored him and stood in front of the dresser mirror, looking at herself. Her face was noticeably older, but still pretty. Her figure remained slender, but physics had a way of making everything more… droopy than she remembered.

How did time go by so fast? she thought to herself. How long has Henry been away from our home, living in that *dirty* city? How long has he been caught up in *their* world, with *her*?

She opened the dresser drawer and quickly changed into her night blouse. She turned to look if Arthur was looking as she did, but he wasn't. He had already picked up a book from the nightstand and was lying in bed, reading where he left off.

This was her life now.

She had nothing unless Henry was here, with her.

What did the city folk call it? *Empty nest syndrome*? She smiled to herself.

She reached into the dresser drawer and grabbed a yellow envelope. She took her time sliding out the photos inside.

She stopped when she heard laughter from Henry's room. Listen to them snickering like little children, she thought to herself. She took out a photo. She stared at the photo of Chelsea, before she was married to Henry. It was a candid shot of her walking across the street. She had no clue the picture was taken, but despite that looked like a model positioning herself just right for the perfect photo.

She really was *pretty*, Martha thought. Wholesome even. Shy, but with a redeemable character to her. She could see why Henry asked for her hand in marriage. He didn't know everything though. Martha had seen girls like her before.

She pulled out another photo from the envelope. She took her time looking at the pretty face staring back at her. It was another candid shot, but this time Carrie Sanders.

She was pretty too – once.

Martha grabbed another photo. This time it was not a candid shot but one with Henry with his arm wrapped around Carrie's shoulder. Carrie had her fingers raised with an emerald ring proudly showing. The picture was taken at the cabin the night they were engaged. Martha smiled to herself seeing how happy Carrie was.

Happiness never lasts. Carrie found that out the hard way.

Carrie was a nice girl, and so is Chelsea. Carrie was happy once, but not anymore. *Happiness never lasts.* She wondered when Chelsea would learn this lesson and didn't mind speeding up her education.

Martha looked back at her husband lying in the bed, unaware of her presence. Everyone finds out that lesson in life. Some only find out years later though. Chelsea would find out much sooner.

Martha felt a tear forming. She quickly wiped it away.

"Stop being so dramatic," Arthur said from the side of his mouth, turning the page. "And put those away."

Martha didn't listen right away. She looked at the pictures again of Carrie and Chelsea, before stuffing them back into the envelope and sliding it into the dresser drawer. She slipped into the bedsheets and stared at the ceiling. Her mind was racing with ideas.

"When do you think she will figure it out?" she asked her husband.

Arthur shrugged, his eyes still glued to the pages of his book. Martha knew his thriller was likely entertaining but was getting annoyed with him.

"It doesn't matter anymore," Arthur finally responded. He looked up at Martha and lowered his reading glasses. "You still haven't told Henry though, right?"

Martha smiled. "In good time."

CHAPTER NINE

"He's *sick*?" Chelsea repeated.

Henry lowered his head. "I worry that it's early Alzheimer's. He's only sixty-five, but lately he's... *different*. He's also forgetting things, many things lately."

Chelsea palmed his chin and caressed the side of his face. She could feel his tear on her hand, and she wiped it away. Henry rarely cried. He was always the rock, while she wept. It was weird to see him so... vulnerable. While she was sad for him, she couldn't help but feel more connected in that moment.

"What kind of things is he forgetting?" Chelsea asked.

"Well... it seems small, but he knows my company's name. I was worried that he forgot about your parents for a moment at dinner too. Mom says he has been calling her different names of women she doesn't even know. One night, she caught him in the living room, a handgun on his lap, staring at the front door. Mom locks up the guns now, and most of the large knives after using them."

Chelsea felt unsettled for a moment, thinking about a large, timid man like Arthur doing such a thing. It was hard for her to picture the jolly man she'd met today acting in such a way.

"Has he been to a doctor yet?" she asked.

Henry smiled to himself. "Do you really think my parents are the type to see one? They don't even own a car." He gestured around the cabin. "*This* is their life. This is all they ever wanted. They don't want to leave it. He would never leave it. Do you know how much my parents have tried to stop me from *leaving* here? Every time I visit, they come up with reasons for me to stay. I have to pry them off me before I leave. Just wait – you'll see it for yourself soon enough." Henry raised his head. "He *won't* see a doctor, but that's part of why I'm here this weekend. I wanted to see how he was doing for myself, and if it's truly as bad as mom says it is, try and convince him to come with us when we leave back to the city. We could try and get him in to see a doctor at a hospital or something."

Chelsea kissed the side of his face. "My grandma had Alzheimer's. She was in her mid-seventies when she was diagnosed. It was terrible. They were able to give her medicine which delayed her disease, and..." Chelsea didn't finish her thought on purpose. She could see the hurt in Henry's face and didn't want to tell him the truth. It destroyed who her grandma was until she finally passed and was at peace. "Your dad seems like a *good* person. Maybe together we can try and convince him."

Henry looked down again. Chelsea waited for him to respond, but he took his time. "You know the worst part? I like him *more-* now." Henry wiped a tear from his eye and turned his face away. "You keep saying how nice he is, and from how he is *now* I would agree. He wasn't always like this. Before, well, I *hated* him. I hated my own father for a long time."

Chelsea put her head on his shoulder. She recognized Henry had a lot to say, and she wanted to let him know she was there for him, and to listen to every word he uttered.

Henry reached around and played with her hair. "He would beat me – us. Mom too. One time, I stood up to him when I was a teenager. That was... a *bad* idea." Henry laughed to himself. "Now that he may be sick, he's different. *Nicer.*"

Chelsea remembered her grandma near the end. When her memory deteriorated, she had become more volatile. She was quick to temper and had even socked her grandpa in the mouth in her confusion. Chelsea kept that comment to herself though. There would be a time to help Henry understand what Arthur was going through, after doctors confirmed his diagnosis.

Henry turned and looked at her. "Sea, is it wrong? I like

my father more now that he's... *sick*."

Chelsea kissed his cheek again softly. "No, you're not bad for thinking that way. I didn't know anything about this, about your father. I'm sorry."

Henry smirked. "How do you do that?"

Chelsea gave a thin smile back. "What?"

"How do you make me feel like we're the only two people in the world right now? I really love you."

"I love you, too." She kissed his forehead.

He took her arm and kissed her wrist. As he did, her sleeve rolled up and she could see one of the many marks on her skin. She quickly rolled her sleeve back down.

"Are you okay?" Henry asked.

"Just... self conscious about it, you know, being at your parents' house."

Henry nodded. "I get it, but that's not *you* anymore. You're strong now, better."

While she hadn't cut herself in a long time – basically since meeting Henry – his words came off to her as fake. *Strong* would be the last word she would use to describe herself. Weak, pitiful, shy. These were better words.

They kissed each other again before getting into the sheets. Henry spooned her for less than ten minutes before he passed out. She always hated that about him. How the hell could he sleep so easily? It was as if someone shot him with a tranquilizer every night when he put his head down on the pillow.

Chelsea was different. She could take hours going to sleep some nights. She loved the affection Henry gave her, even at night. It did give her a sense of security, but after he fell asleep, she always wanted to shove him off her. She needed her space to roll around and find the right spot. Sometimes in their apartment, she would put a sleeping app on her phone to help her drift away. It sometimes helped – but many times it wouldn't, though.

She knew she was going to struggle with sleeping before

she came to her in-laws' home and wished she had thought of more ways to help.

Henry started breathing more heavily. It wasn't exactly a snore, but it wasn't a normal breath either. It was somewhere in between.

Chelsea tried to shut her eyes and force herself to sleep for what felt like forever. Eventually she opened them again, feeling annoyed at each breath Henry made on her shoulder. She looked around the near pitch-dark room. The only light came from the moon through the opening in the curtains. The dim light highlighted her bare arm stretched out on the bed. Even in the dark, she could see one of the marks on her wrist.

A sense of shame hit her like a ton of bricks. She imagined what her mother-in-law would say to her if she saw this mark and the others Chelsea had made on herself. Chelsea wasn't as scared about what Martha would say to her face but more what she would say to Henry.

"This is the woman you chose?" she could hear her mother-in-law say.

Chelsea nearly rolled her eyes when she realized she was scratching her wrist again. It was something she knew she did when she was stressed. It was better than cutting herself but sometimes she would scratch a little *too* hard.

Chelsea slowly untangled herself from Henry and rolled out of bed quietly. She grabbed her phone from the nightstand and attempted to leave the bedroom without making noise, but the old wood floors made it nearly impossible. Every step she made had a different creak.

When she left the bedroom, she closed the door halfway. The hallway was pitch black. She clicked on her phone and pointed it at Henry's parents' door. It remained shut, thankfully. She turned her phone the other way and put on her flashlight. She made her way to the front door.

In their apartment, some nights when Chelsea would struggle with sleeping, she would sit outside on the balcony and listen to the city sounds. Living in downtown Calgary, the streets always had something going on. The sirens, people shouting from the bars below or cars passing. It made her feel like she wasn't the only one not sleeping.

When she got closer to the front door, she noticed the red light above was on. She cursed to herself, remembering that Henry said the security system locked them inside at night. She looked outside the window beside the front door. The woods were dark and still.

She spotted a red-light reflection in the window and was confused. She looked up at the red panel shining brightly above the door and realized it wasn't that. She turned around and in the darkness of the living room spotted a red light from near the fire mantle.

Is that a camera? Chelsea thought to herself.

The sound of a howl broke her concentration. She quickly looked outside the window again, trying to find the source.

"God damn wolf!"

Chelsea turned back to the living room and saw a shadowy figure moving back and forth. She shined her light and saw Arthur sitting on a fabric rocking chair. For a moment she was struck with fear. She quickly moved the light around her father-in-law, focusing on his lap and hands. Then she remembered what Henry said about them locking away his guns.

Arthur raised his arms, covering his face. "Could you lower that?" he asked softly. Chelsea quickly turned her phone away. "I must have slept in my chair again," Arthur said with a laugh. "Are you okay?"

Chelsea smiled. "Oh, yeah. I just wanted some water."

Arthur smiled back. In the darkness, it came off more menacing than it did during the daytime. "Well, you won't find clean water out there," he said pointing outside the window. "Let me help you." He stood up from his chair with a groan and slowly made his way to the fridge. When he opened the door, it illuminated the room and he seemed less nefarious.

He grabbed a pitcher from the fridge and two glasses

from a cabinet above. He poured water in both and gave one to her. He raised the glass in his hand. "I hope we're not too much for you."

Chelsea lowered her head and grabbed her glass, taking a sip. "No, of course not."

Arthur smiled again. "Meeting the parents is always *scary*. Was for me back in the day at least."

Chelsea smiled back. "Well, a *little*, I guess." She remembered Henry's words about his father but couldn't see the brutal man he'd described. His face had wrinkles on the side that were made larger with every smile. It was as if the man had been smiling his whole life.

"But you're not so scared now?" he asked.

Outside, the wolf howled again and it made her jump. Arthur laughed. "I guess I'd be more scared if I was out there."

Arthur's smile faded. He glanced down the dark hallway at the bedroom doors. "Do you know how to get back to the highway from here?" He looked back at her sternly.

Chelsea was taken aback by his question and sudden change in demeanor. Before she could answer, she heard the creak of a door opening followed by footsteps coming down the dark hallway.

"Arthur?" Martha called out. "Is that you?"

"Just helping Chelsea get some water," he answered. "I slept in my chair again."

Martha was barely visible, but she could see her hand gesturing for Arthur to come with her. "Let's go to bed, Arthur."

Arthur nodded. "Goodnight, Chelsea." He started walking down the hall, and together their footsteps creaked all the way back to their bedroom.

"Good night, Arthur, and Mar— Mrs. Jameson," Chelsea called out. In the darkness she could hear their door close. She took another sip of water and stared outside. Maybe she was better outside with the wolf after all.

Henry had said it was his father he'd feared, but Chelsea couldn't figure out how to get in his mother's good graces, if such a thing was even possible. She didn't know what she wanted more, to get along with her in-laws, or leave their home.

CHAPTER TEN

Chelsea snuck back under the covers with Henry once she was certain that Martha and Arthur were not coming back out of their bedroom. Henry rolled over and slowly opened his eyes.

"You, okay?" he asked. "Can't sleep?"

Chelsea laid her head on the pillow and looked at Henry's brown eyes, taking in the way he looked at her. "I guess I can't get over how we're in the middle of nowhere. I'm not used to it."

Henry smiled. "My city-slicker girl. The wolf howling woke me up too, but don't worry."

"I feel like this weekend isn't going the way you want it," Chelsea admitted. "The way I want it."

Henry caressed her face. "What do you mean?"

"I mean, I feel like your mom *hates* me."

Henry scoffed. "No, of course not. She's just... *different*. It's not about you."

"She never met me before we married. I wonder what she would have said to you if she had?"

Henry waved his head. "She would have congratulated me for making the best decision I've ever made." Somehow, Chelsea felt those wouldn't be her actual words.

"I guess..." She thought of her dad for a moment. "I was hoping I could be part of a new family. Yours. I see how much they love you. I miss that feeling."

"My mom, she will come around, believe me. Dad already likes you. I can tell."

"I was talking to your dad for a little," she said.

Henry sat up against the headboard. "Was he *okay*?"

"Yeah, I think so. He slept in his rocking chair. I woke him, I think. I was a little *freaked* out though..." She thought of the weird question Arthur asked her before Martha came into the room. She also thought of the red light of what looked like a camera in the living room.

"What did he say?"

"Is that a camera in the living room?" she asked.

Henry rolled his eyes. "Yep, *weird*, right? I told you how Dad has been lately. After the gun incident I had one put in just to make sure everything was okay. If I saw something strange, I could take it to the doctors." He paused for a moment. "Mom's worried he is going to start wandering in the night outside too. The security system helps with that now, though."

Chelsea thought about what it must be like for Martha living with Arthur as his memory got worse. Chelsea would be afraid. She wouldn't be able to live in the middle of nowhere while someone got sicker.

"How does your mom stay out here like this while your dad gets worse?" she asked.

Henry shrugged. "I've had those conversations myself with her. She's more stubborn than Dad. She finds ways to deal with it. If Dad says something weird, she'll usually ignore it, or play along until he drops whatever it is he's going on about." He took a deep breath. "I'm hoping they come to their senses, though. It would be hard to drag the old man back to the highway, but whatever it takes."

That made her think of what Arthur said before leaving. "There was something else," she said. "He asked me a question. I guess... it wasn't a weird one, but his expression made it seem that way. He—"

A thud on the wall made her stop talking. She was about to tell Henry to go check what made that sound when she felt another, and worried that somehow Arthur had fallen and was hurt. Then a whispered moan of a man made her realize what was *really* happening. She looked at Henry in shock.

A creak of the bed in the other room made Henry's eyes

widen. "Oh no," he muttered.

Chelsea curled in the bed in horror. She could hear the whispered moaning of Martha now, and the creaking sounds getting faster.

She covered her face with a pillow. "This *can't* be happening right now."

"Well, like you said, they live in the middle of nowhere. Not exactly used to having guests."

"Please *god*," Chelsea said to the ceiling. "Make it stop."

"Should I knock on the wall?" Henry said with a smile. "Tell them to keep it down in there or something?" He raised a hand, and Chelsea quickly grabbed it.

"No, that will make it worse. They will know that we heard." She breathed in.

Henry laughed quietly. "I mean, I feel terrible right now, but on the other hand happy that my parents are still, you know, *getting it on.*"

Chelsea hit him in the shoulder. "Stop!" She quickly lowered her voice and hit him again. "Stop it." Chelsea put the pillow over her head and tried to cover her ears.

"How much longer do you think they have in them?" Henry said.

Chelsea let out a feigned crying sound. "Not long, for my *sanity.*"

If this weekend became any more awkward, she would die.

CHAPTER ELEVEN

Chelsea woke up, the sun blinding her through the sheer curtains. She wasn't sure what time it was, but she had been woken up by a rooster several times already this morning. Henry somehow slept through all the farm noises. She guessed he was the opposite of her: the city life comforted her to sleep while the farm helped him. She supposed it didn't matter where they were; Henry would always have better sleep than her.

When she opened her eyes, Henry wasn't beside her this time. She could hear people talking in the hall and took a deep breath.

"It's only a weekend," she reminded herself. She made a mental note that today was Saturday and felt glee that tomorrow they would be leaving. While feeling overcome with joy thinking about it, she also felt shame. Wasn't there an expectation to be able to get along with the in-laws?

She didn't exactly *not get* along with them, but felt uneasy. She felt like she didn't belong. Henry, on the other hand, seemed happy to be back, but of course he would; they were his parents.

Chelsea stretched her arms out, yawning. She grabbed her phone from the nightstand and noticed it was only seven thirty in the morning. When she stood up from the bed, she could feel the stickiness of her shirt that clung to her back. She must have sweated off five pounds, which didn't leave much Chelsea left. Even in their condo in Calgary she wore long sleeves, though, and couldn't bear the idea of not doing so. Arthur was right, though, the home heated up and kept the heat through the night.

On a bookshelf close by, she noticed pictures between books sticking out. She couldn't help herself and slipped one of them out. The first one was of Henry with his arm wrapped around a woman Chelsea didn't recognise. She noticed a large emerald ring on her finger.

Chelsea knew instantly that the mystery woman was likely the infamous Carrie Sanders. She quickly put the picture back between the books, not wanting to look at her. It wasn't that she was upset that Henry had dated before her. Of course he had. She worried that she would examine Carrie and wonder why Henry chose her over his ex.

The next picture was a little baby boy in blue overalls next to a large pumpkin. The child was obviously Henry. Even at such a young age he'd mastered the smirk.

She smiled. If Henry and her did have children, they would be beautiful. That was the first question Henry asked when they started dating seriously: "Do you want children?"

It was important for him to be a father. Chelsea appreciated how he didn't beat around the bush with what he wanted in a relationship. Chelsea at times wanted a child or two herself at times. She worried that she wasn't *mother material*. She thought of Martha. No matter how harsh she came off, you knew she had Henry's side. It didn't matter if Henry was wrong or right, Martha would always have her son's back, like a lioness. Chelsea admired her for that.

One of the books on his shelf caught her eye. *How to Win Friends and Influence People*. She picked it up and skimmed through a few pages.

A self-help book? she thought to herself. Below it was a book about cognitive behavioural therapy. Henry did not come off like the type to need these types of books to help him. He had always seemed so confident and caring. She didn't consider that he must have his own demons that he fought. Chelsea felt ashamed of herself. Her whole relationship, Henry had been catering to her and her needs, but Chelsea never looked out for him. He was there for her when her father died. He was there for her when she grieved. He understood her when she told him about the cutting.

Have I ever let Henry lean on me? she thought. She never knew about how his father hurt him and his mother. She never knew about the struggles he and his family had.

She would change that. This weekend, as painful and awkward as it could be for her at times, was the opportunity for her to really understand her husband.

Chelsea quietly opened the door and spotted Henry and his mother talking further down the hallway, closer to the kitchen. They hadn't noticed Chelsea yet and were engrossed in their conversation.

Chelsea was about to greet them when Henry said loudly, "Just stop it. Stop. I've had enough of this."

"You don't know, do you?" Martha said in a harsh tone. "Can she even give you a child? Have you seen a doctor? How do you know she can?"

"It doesn't matter," Henry said. "She's my *wife*."

"I know what a child means to you, Henry. I do."

Chelsea could feel her heart sink. She wished she was invisible. She wished she'd never taken the epic hike to be here with Henry. She wished she could have told Henry she was too busy with getting ready for art school to come this weekend to meet his parents, or any other excuse she could have thought to use. Most of all, she wanted to scream at the top of her lungs at his mother.

"Good morning."

Chelsea turned and saw Arthur closing his bedroom door.

Chelsea fully opened the bedroom door and closed it behind her. "Morning."

Henry waved at her, and Martha managed to feign a smile. Chelsea wanted to bolt between Henry and Martha and run out the front door, through the woods and back into town in her pajamas.

Instead, she managed a smile herself. "Good morning,

Martha."

"Henry and I are going fishing after breakfast," Arthur said. "Want to join?"

"I love fishing. My dad taught me when I was younger. I haven't been in a long time, though."

"Not a problem," Arthur said. "Henry and I can show you anything you forgot."

Martha cleared her throat. "Actually, I need some help." Martha came up to Chelsea. "Let the boys hunt. We can gather. There's work to do in the garden."

Chelsea wished she could come up with something witty to avoid any alone time with Martha but couldn't find the words. She wanted to tell her mother-in-law what she had just heard hurt her in more ways than she could know. She wanted to *tell her off*.

Instead, Chelsea nodded. "I'd love to."

CHAPTER TWELVE

Chelsea picked raspberries from a bush, taking her time. Martha was a row ahead of her, grabbing berries quickly and placing them in a wicker basket. The faster Chelsea went, the closer she would be to her mother-in-law. After what Martha had said to Henry this morning, Chelsea could feel anger reaching a height she'd never felt with anyone before.

As she thought about Martha, she realized her grip on a berry was too tight, squishing it in her palm. She discarded it discreetly so Martha wouldn't see. She glanced at her mother-in-law picking berries. Raspberry picking was supposed to be fun, but despite her beautiful sundress, dark apron over it and large hat, even now she looked moody. Her thick eyebrows were furrowed as she picked berries and her bottom lip was tight.

Resting bitch face was the term for it, and Martha wore it with pride. Chelsea would never use the term to describe someone, but if ever she did, now would be perfect.

Chelsea stared off into a patch of bushes away from the garden. Nearly an hour ago Henry and Arthur had walked off together in that direction, fishing rods in hand. She wished she could have gone with them. Instead – she looked back at Martha, and back at the raspberry bush – she was here.

Great.

She reached for another berry, catching her sleeve on a branch. She felt the end of the stick poke into her forearm. She tried to wrestle the bush off her sleeve, managing to expose her wrist. With the sun beating down on her, it revealed a large scar. She panicked and managed to untangle herself from the bush and push her sleeve down her arm, covering it.

Martha was staring at her. Chelsea sighed to herself, quietly. She plucked another berry and heard movement. Her mother-in-law was walking towards her.

Chelsea stared down at the bush and plucked another raspberry. She could hear Martha still walking towards her but did not want to look. Keep it together, she thought. It's only a weekend. Chelsea managed a smile and looked up towards Martha.

Her smile vanished quickly.

Martha reached into a pocket in her apron, taking out a Swiss army knife. She opened the blade and continued to walk slowly towards her.

Chelsea panicked for a moment. She covered her eyes from the sun and looked at her mother-in-law coming towards her with the knife. She thought for a moment she saw her grinning.

"Martha?" Chelsea managed. She could feel her heart beat quicker. Chelsea dropped the wicker basket, spilling berries in the dirt.

Martha bent over a few feet in front of her, digging her knife into the ground at the base of a green plant. She wiggled the knife around, thrusting it deeper, and yanked out a large root.

Martha hung the plant in her hand. "*Weeds.* I can't stand them in my garden. They don't belong here." She wiped the knife on her apron, folded it and put it back into her pocket. Martha looked down at the spilt berries. "Are you getting the hang of it?" she asked Chelsea.

"Yeah, of course," Chelsea said. She knelt and picked up the basket, grabbing the fallen berries quickly. "Henry took me berry picking once, at a local farm." Somehow, she remembered it being more fun picking berries than it was today. She kept that comment to herself.

"You have to pick the right ones, though," Martha said. She reached out and grabbed Chelsea's basket. At the force of

Martha tugging on it, Chelsea let go of the handle, allowing her mother-in-law to inspect. Martha shook her head. "Some of these are a little green. The salad doesn't taste nice if you pick the wrong berries. Don't worry – I'll show you how." Martha looked at the bush Chelsea was taking berries from. She squinted and reached in, grabbing a few. Martha opened her hand, showing them to Chelsea. "These ones are perfect. A beautiful red color to them."

Chelsea felt a rush of her heart beating again. Why was picking berries so scary suddenly? What would Martha say to her if she picked the wrong one again? How much more stressful could berry picking get?

Chelsea looked carefully, grabbing one from a bush in front of her. She opened her palm for Martha to analyze. Martha nodded.

"That's better, but you can choose more than one at a time." Martha laughed. Chelsea smiled and laughed as well.

The two of them began picking berries side by side. Chelsea waited for Martha to make another comment, something nasty towards her, but she didn't. They picked fruit in peace. Every so often, Chelsea looked around at the mountains surrounding them and took in the fresh air.

"So," Chelsea said, breaking the silence, "how long have you and Arthur been together?"

"Lost count now."

"Wow," Chelsea said, even though Henry had told her the answer to this question before they came. "That's a long time. You'll have to give me tips." She thought about how she'd *heard* Martha and Arthur last night being intimate. Chelsea could barely keep her hands to herself around Henry but figured at some point that would change. Isn't that how marriage works? She was genuinely interested in how Martha and Arthur stayed interested in each other romantically all these years. Maybe she could learn a few things from her mother-in-law after all, besides picking the right berry.

Martha smiled. "You just have to remember why you love

them to begin with. That's... not always easy to do." Martha plucked a few more berries and tossed them into Chelsea's basket. "How will you be without Henry, when you go to art school?"

Chelsea took a deep breath. "It's going to be hard. I'm going to miss him, a lot. I'll visit him on breaks, or maybe, if business ever slows down for him, he will come see me for a week or two."

"Is it really worth it, though?"

Chelsea lowered her head. "It is to me. I've always wanted to paint professionally."

"Why do you need to go to school for it? I could pick up a paintbrush and start now. Why leave your husband to another province for something you can do anywhere?"

Chelsea could feel her blood boiling. "I'd rather not talk about it. Henry is okay with me going." It had taken Henry some time before he realized how much she loved painting. The first time she visited her father's home and she took Henry into her childhood bedroom, he was taken back with how there wasn't a bare spot on her bedroom walls. Everything was covered with different pictures that she'd painted.

It was a way for her to express herself freely. She could do or say whatever she wanted when she put a paintbrush on a canvas. Chelsea never worried about who she was when she painted. She could stroke her brush across the canvas any way she chose. Nothing stopped her when she had a brush in her hand. Not the scars on her arm, her father's sickness, nothing. She was full of emotions when she painted, but all of them were beautiful. None of them held her back. The only time she felt strong as a person was when she painted.

"I wasn't trying to be rude," Martha said. "Henry told me how much you love to paint. I guess it's hard for me to imagine being away from my husband for so long. I couldn't imagine what that would be like."

Chelsea picked another berry. She managed to keep a smile on her face.

"Henry didn't tell me about your mother, though," Martha said, plucking one berry off the bush. "That she passed when you were so little. That must have been hard." Chelsea maintained her focus on plucking berries. "It was hard for me." Martha plucked another berry off the bush, eating it. "My father died when I was a teenager. To this day, it impacts me in ways I can't explain."

Chelsea looked at Martha now and could see what appeared to be a tear forming in her mother-in-law's eye. She thought she was imagining it at first, but Martha quickly wiped it away.

"It's funny how thinking of him can still get to me even after all these years," Martha said. "Henry, he didn't tell you, I take it?"

Chelsea waved her head. "No, he didn't." He hasn't said much of anything about his family at all really, she thought. "What happened?"

Martha ate a few more berries, lowering her head. "It's still hard for me to talk about. I'm not sure if I can right now."

Chelsea reached out and put her arm on her shoulder. "Of course, that's okay." She'd understood that feeling quite well her whole life.

"I hate to admit this, but I was pretty lost after he died," Martha continued. "Then Henry came into my life." She looked at Chelsea with a wide smile. "Things were better after that. There was a purpose for me. I never knew what love was."

"Henry was there for me when my dad was passing and eventually left. He has a wonderful power of being able to make you feel better after terrible things happen."

Martha laughed. "Well said. Well said. He does though. Maybe you can understand now why that's why I want the *best* for him." Chelsea smiled back. "That's why I worry if the right person for him is *you*."

Chelsea furrowed her eyebrows, wondering if she'd heard her right. She looked at Martha, who stared back at her sternly. Chelsea bit her lip, and tried to manage to keep her smile, but her body resisted.

"Well, you're a little too late for that, Martha," Chelsea said. "We're *already* married."

Martha furrowed her eyebrows. "*What* did you say?"

Chelsea could feel the emotions stirring inside her. It was almost as if she was painting right now. She could feel the anger inside about to explode. It was as if she had dipped her paintbrush in red paint and was about to go crazy on a canvas with it.

"Hey!" Henry yelled to them. He walked into the garden, waving. Chelsea spotted Arthur limping behind him. "Mom, can you come over here?"

Martha looked at Chelsea for a moment. "Of course, dear!" She stood up and walked towards them, grabbing the wicker basket of berries.

"I just want to talk to my parents quickly," Henry called out to Chelsea.

Take your time, Chelsea thought to herself. She plucked a berry and tossed it in her mouth. She had plucked the wrong one. It was green, too sour, but she didn't care.

CHAPTER THIRTEEN

Henry *saves the day* again, Chelsea thought to herself. She watched as her husband gathered his mother and father into what looked like a football huddle. She wondered what they were talking about, but after the conversation she'd had with Martha, she couldn't care less.

She felt a buzz in her jean pocket. She slipped out her phone and smiled when she saw Neil was calling her.

"Hey," she said, answering the call.

"Hey yourself," Neil said with a laugh. "You haven't been texting me back, I was getting worried."

"Nothing to worry about," Chelsea said. "Except my *sanity.*"

"Is it that *bad*?"

"Worse. I can't believe it's only been a day and a half."

"I mean, this is coming from you of all people," Neil said with a chuckle. "The room could literally be on fire, and you'd be stuck in the middle of it saying, 'It's fine.' So, it must be hell."

"It's only for the *weekend*," Chelsea said as if it was Henry saying it to her.

"Sure," Neil said. "Plus an *eternity.* Nobody tells you when you get married that you will marry the family also."

"Well, I never met the family until now. I don't think I can take them back." Chelsea started walking across the garden, giving herself more distance from Henry and his family.

"Where are you? I thought these people live in the middle of nowhere?"

"They do. We had to hike four hours to get here.

Somehow, I get cell phone bars in certain areas."

"Say that again," Neil said. "You're breaking up."

"I said—"

"I can't hear you."

Flustered, Chelsea raised her voice. "Can you hear me?" Neil started laughing. Chelsea laughed too. "Stop messing with me." She peeked over her shoulder and saw Martha staring at her. "Please stop messing with me," she repeated.

"Okay, okay," Neil said. "But I mean, you sound pretty fed up. I can't imagine Henry's parents would be that bad."

Chelsea quickly thought about some of the highlights of the weekend. It was much worse, she thought to herself. "Well, the father isn't so bad, but his mom, she's from a different *planet*."

"Can you say that again?" Neil said.

"Ugh. Can you stop Neil. I'm not in the mood for this."

"No, that time you did cut o—" Neil's voice was disjointed this time.

Chelsea moved further into the garden, getting even further away from her in-laws. "Can you hear me now?"

"That's better," Neil said.

"We leave tomorrow, hopefully right away. I'll be seeing you soon. I'll tell you all about it."

"You bring a bottle of wine," Neil said. "I'll bring a case of beers."

"Did you want to get together Tuesday?"

"That works. We need to book a flight. I emailed the landlord of that apartment we were looking at, and he wants to Zoom chat with us when we can, to get to know us."

Chelsea looked out into the garden at Henry, who was still talking to his parents. "Maybe we should do this at your place."

Neil let out an audible sigh. "You didn't tell him, did you?" Chelsea didn't answer. "C'mon, Chelz. Do you really think he is going to care that much? You're a married woman."

"I told him I was looking for a roommate," she said at a whisper. "I mean, he still hates the idea of me going, and he's not the biggest fan of you coming with me. I want to tell him when we get back. This trip is already bad enough."

"He's met me," Neil said. "What does he think I'm going to do if we live together? We need to save money somehow."

Chelsea remembered the first night Henry had met Neil. The three of them went out to a brewery at Neil's recommendation. Neil was being himself, funny, witty. Neil and Chelsea had built up many inside jokes over the years of their friendship, and that night it felt like he put them all out on display for Henry. Chelsea had to keep explaining what they were talking about because it was almost like speaking in code. Chelsea didn't think Neil was being rude. That's just how he was. He liked to reminisce.

Henry said he liked him that night. He didn't like the idea that Neil had been engaged previously, though. He thought it showed immaturity, that he couldn't follow through with his promise to wed.

Chelsea walked further into the garden. "I don't know what Henry's thinking," Chelsea said to Neil. "I just don't want to upset him more with me leaving. I will tell him, soon."

"We should be leaving this week. We have to. There's still so much to figure out."

"I'll—"

"Chelz, you're breaking up again."

Chelsea moved across the field until Neil confirmed he could hear her. "I will tell him," Chelsea repeated.

Chelsea felt an arm wrap around her shoulder and hang from her side. She jumped until she realized it was Henry.

"What's that?" Henry said.

Chelsea composed herself. "Hey," she said.

"That Neil on the phone?" Henry said. He lowered his head near her cell. "Hey, Neil!" he yelled. "Surprised you can even talk to him out here."

"Let me just say bye," Chelsea said. She picked up the cell to her ear. "Hey," she said to Neil.

"Fuck, did he hear you?" Neil whispered. "Tell him how

much you hate it there. Tell him you hate your mother-in-law. Tell him you're hiking all the way back to town." Neil laughed.

Chelsea shook her head but maintained a smile for Henry. "See you Tuesday." She hung up and slipped her phone in her pocket.

"*Tuesday*? Henry repeated.

"We're just getting our plans ready for Toronto. Figuring a few things out."

"Gotcha," Henry said with a smirk.

"What is it?" Chelsea asked.

"Nothing," Henry said. "I mean, I know he's a nice guy…"

"But?"

"The guy is *totally* into you."

"Henry, please don't do this again. We're friends; that's it. We have always been friends, since… forever."

"The way he talks to you is the way I'd talk to you, to get your attention."

"Henry, you have nothing to worry about with Neil. You know that. You trust me, right?"

Henry nodded. "That doesn't mean I trust him. Let me ask you this. If you were to tell him you wanted to get with him, what would he say? What would he do if you were interested in him, right now? Would he hesitate a minute to think about it?"

Chelsea made a face of disgust. "Can we not even imagine that scenario? I would never do that."

"Fine. What if he came onto you, stronger than he already is? What if he flat out told you he wanted to be with you, what would you say?"

"No," Chelsea said firmly.

"What would happen after?"

Chelsea shrugged. "I guess it depends. If he wouldn't stop, that would be the end of our friendship."

Henry smiled. "*Good.* I just wanted to hear that. I feel better now. I'll drop the jealous husband act."

"Some *act* you have there. You know I love you more than anything."

Henry grabbed her hips and brought her closer to him. "I know." He kissed her softly on the lips. "But maybe you won't love me *much* longer."

"What's wrong?"

Henry took a deep breath and put out his hands as if he was an escaped prisoner being caught by the police. "Okay, so things are blowing up on that big project at work. I got a text from James, about the Highland project. The buyer is having issues with the quote I gave them. They say things aren't adding up correctly. It's sort of a big deal."

"Can't James fix it?"

"No," Henry said firmly. "I made the quote. James doesn't know how I come up with those figures. I don't want him to mess up and give them an amount that makes them scratch their heads more. I need to go back and fix my numbers and send it to them right away. It will only take a few hours once I'm there."

"So we need to leave?" Chelsea said.

"I'll hike it back to the truck. With any luck I'll be able to make it back before it gets too dark. Worst case, I'll be back in the morning."

Chelsea furrowed her eyebrows. "You mean you want me to *stay* while you leave? No, Henry—"

"Listen," Henry said at a whisper. "I know this weekend hasn't been going as well as hoped, but how would it look if we both left? This is the last good weekend before you leave. I promised them to stay the whole weekend. It would look bad if we both left."

"Henry," Chelsea said sternly. "I heard you and your mom this morning. "Can she even have children?" Chelsea repeated in a stern voice, mimicking Martha. "I heard that. I can't—"

"I'm sorry you heard that," Henry cut in. "Mom can be a lot, I know. She just wants—"

"What's *best* for you," Chelsea finished. "I know, she just told me that."

Henry smiled. "Good. So she talked to you? I told her to

try and clear the air with you."

Chelsea shook her head. "She doesn't think I'm good for you."

Henry put his head down. "I'm trying my best, Sea, I am. I want you and my parents to get along. I worry about my dad. I wanted to keep an extra eye on him to see what other issues he's having. I thought you could help me figure out a way to help him. Now I need to fix this issue for business. I mean, someone has to pay for your Toronto adventure." Henry's voice was more stern than usual.

Chelsea's eyes began to water. Henry immediately saw it and apologized.

"That's not fair," Chelsea said. "Can you not do that to me?"

Henry put his hands up. "Sorry, Sea. I didn't mean to come off like that. I'm just still having a hard time with you going. I know I'll be able to see you." Henry lowered his head. "The stress this weekend has been too much."

On that they could agree. "You promise you will be back tonight?" she asked.

Henry smirked. "I'll do everything I can to get back today."

Chelsea nodded. "Fine, I'll stay. I'll watch over your father."

"I owe you big time, Sea."

Chelsea hit his chest with her fist playfully. "Yes, you do." They kissed again. Chelsea thought of Neil. She wondered how well Henry would take the news when she shared it.

CHAPTER FOURTEEN

Henry packed his bag full of snacks and water for the hike. Before leaving, he embraced Chelsea one last time, thanking her for staying again. Then he went to his parents, hugging each of them. He whispered something in his mother's ear. Martha noticed Chelsea watching, though, and Chelsea quickly turned her head.

"I should be back tonight!" Henry shouted, waving at Chelsea and his family.

"You sure you don't want to take a gun or a knife with you?" Martha said. "The wolf—"

"I'll be fine, Mom," Henry said. He waved one last time to Chelsea before heading into the bush. Chelsea blew a kiss at him, but he hadn't noticed. He was already getting deep into the bush to where she couldn't even make out his figure. It was almost as if the woods sucked Henry into them.

Chelsea looked at Arthur and Martha a moment, then down at the ground. *Now what?* she thought to herself.

"Well, we should probably finish gardening," Martha said. Chelsea managed a smile but inside felt torn. She wanted anything but to complete the last conversation they had.

"I could use an extra hand at fishing," Arthur said. "We didn't catch anything. Henry was busy with his business emergency, so we don't have much of a meal. I could use an extra rod in the water."

Martha scowled, but before she could resist Chelsea piped up. "That sounds great."

Arthur waved towards the barn. "We can grab the rods. I

left the bait bucket at the riverbank."

Martha discreetly left and went back inside the cabin. Chelsea noticed her glancing at her and Arthur before closing the front door behind her.

"Well, let's go," Arthur said. He limped down the dirt path towards the barn and Chelsea followed, matching his pace.

"Are you much of a fisher?" Arthur asked. "You said you were in Girl Guides, right?"

"My father took me a lot when I was younger," she answered. She did have fond memories of her and her father going to Bow River in Calgary. The river offered some of the best fly fishing in the world, but she never learned to fish that way. "My dad, he never depended on it like you do. He would mostly catch and release his fish."

"Most rivers in Calgary don't allow you to eat what you catch anyways," Arthur said. "We— I mean, I would go all the time to Bow River to fish when I was younger."

"That's where my father went," Chelsea said.

"Could you imagine if we fished the same river at the same time, but never knew? The world is funny like that." Arthur looked back at the house, and at Chelsea. When Arthur was close enough, he reached out for the barn door.

"That would be something," Chelsea agreed. "So how did you and Martha meet?"

Arthur seemed to not hear her as he opened the door with a loud creak. He stepped inside and hit his head playfully. "Ah, I forgot to have Henry help me with the traps. Damn."

"He'll be back soon."

Arthur smiled. "Well, how about you earn another badge for your Girl Guide uniform? Trapping isn't too hard. We won't do the large ones for the wolf. I'll wait for Henry to come back for that. But I'll show you how to do the smaller ones."

"Sure," Chelsea said. "Although they don't have a trapping badge for Girl Guides."

"You'll be ahead of the pack," Arthur said, laughing to himself. He reached up and grabbed a small trap hanging on the wall. "You have the springs on the side." Arthur showed her, brushing his hand against the metal. "And the jaws, or teeth, which are what close in on the animal once it's in your trap. For the larger ones, you open the spring using this." Arthur picked up a large metal bar. "But for the small ones like this, you can use your own hands, carefully." Arthur continued to give her a lesson in off the grid living and Chelsea enjoyed learning from him.

Arthur grabbed another small trap from the wall. "Go ahead, you try." Chelsea followed the steps Arthur showed her and set the trap quickly. "Well, there you go," Arthur said. "We will make an outdoor woman out of you yet." Arthur pointed at the larger traps. "It's the same principle with any trap."

He showed Chelsea how to dismantle the traps. "On the way to the river we can set up a few traps as well, and maybe we'll get lucky and catch a rabbit."

"How often do you trap an animal?" Chelsea asked.

"Every so often. The trick with trapping is you have to give them something they want. Final test for your badge: what is the trick to trap any animal?"

Chelsea laughed. "Trap them by giving them something they want."

Arthur clapped and smiled, stretching the wrinkles on his face. "Excellent." He lowered his head.

"Are you okay?" she asked.

"Nothing. You just remind me of someone." When he raised his head, his eyes appeared a little red. He took out a cloth from his back pocket, blowing his nose. "You know, I always wanted a daughter."

Chelsea smiled again. "Well, I guess you have one now."

Arthur nodded. "I suppose I do." He walked to the other side of the barn and grabbed two fishing rods on the counter. "We should use the rest of our light to get some fish."

CHAPTER FIFTEEN

Martha

They have been away for some time, Martha thought to herself. She looked out into the garden from inside the cabin. He won't stay... *composed*. He's not able to do what's needed.

He didn't see what needed to be done. It was her own fault for leaving Chelsea with him for so long. Arthur wasn't *made* for this.

Chelsea wasn't *made* for this either- but she would find that out the hard way.

Martha sighed. Something might need to be done. This wasn't what was supposed to happen. All she wanted in this world was for Henry to stay. When he came back, she would make sure he did. She would explain *everything* to him.

Chelsea isn't made for this lifestyle. Henry is.

All Martha had to do was explain that to Henry, and he would understand. He wouldn't leave. This time she wouldn't let him. He needed to understand.

They were one *happy* family. No one else needed to join them, not anymore.

Arthur messed that up, Martha thought to herself. How many times had she explained to Arthur what was needed? What was required of him?

He was going to mess this up, Martha knew. Then what? Everything had to change. Henry would try and leave.

That couldn't happen.

He better not have screwed this up, she thought. Martha

was never the type to sit back and wait for something terrible to happen. She wasn't the type to passively wait for everything to fall apart.

Action was needed.

Martha was always one to do what was needed. When she was a little girl and her parents would beat her senseless after school, finding whatever reasons they used to justify it, she made a *plan*. She wasn't going to let them have power over her forever.

She saved every cent she made from a paper route she had for almost six months. She hid cans from the pantry. She kept all her money and food in a bag below a shed in the backyard. She figured out the cost of a bus ticket, and the times they left and to where.

She planned out every step she needed to get away from them, and then put her plan into action. One summer day, when her father was at work at the mill and her mother was at a church function, she would escape.

What she didn't plan for was her father to come home *drunk*, well before quitting time. When he saw her with a bag and an envelope full of cash in her pocket, he tried to stop her.

She didn't plan to hurt him. She just wanted to get away. One moment he was chasing her, the next he tripped and fell in his drunkenness. It was as if something took over her that day. She didn't remember taking a can from her bag, sitting on top of her father and mashing his face with the cold tin until he stopped moving.

Martha was sure that he'd lived, at least, that's what her mind told her to this day. She didn't stay to find out what happened to him. She executed the rest of her plan after cleaning up and changing into new clothes.

She got far away from her parents to a place where they would never hurt her again. She didn't need anybody to help her survive. All she needed was herself. Her wits. Her planning.

Martha had a plan now. Arthur sure as hell didn't know. When the time came to execute her plan, she would. Until then, she would take her time. Doing what was required for her plan to be successful.

Martha furrowed her eyebrows. She'd never considered herself a *monster*. Was that what she was becoming?

No. She was a *survivor*, and would do whatever it took to live, no matter what the cost.

Henry would forgive her and understand, *some day*.

All of her planning would be useless, though, if Arthur messed it up.

Martha quickly ran to her bedroom, grabbed her key from her dresser, and made her way to the shed beside the barn. She opened the lock and the dead bolt with one key on her ring. When she was inside, she switched on a light, turning to a large shelf.

Where is it? she thought. She looked for the tin box she'd bought when she was younger at the 1991 Calgary Stampede, a world-famous rodeo.

Had *he* been inside the shed? Had he moved the tin box? Why?

When had he been inside the shed? Martha thought.

Martha breathed in deep. Arthur had moved the box. He must have. Martha was getting careless with her key. Arthur knew of it. She would keep it around her neck now.

If Chelsea found the box, everything would change.

Worse though, if Arthur had the gun that she kept inside the box, nobody was safe.

CHAPTER SIXTEEN

To her surprise, Chelsea was the first to catch a fish. Arthur helped her reel it in, almost out of desperation that they would have no dinner, but had fun with it. She had caught a medium sized trout. Chelsea laughed, thinking how she caught a fish she would usually buy at a grocery store. It was thrilling.

Arthur was a good teacher, though. He took his time explaining how to reel in a fish once one nibbled on the bait. Arthur was the first to get a bite, but the fish fought hard, nearly pulling him off his feet.

After Chelsea napped the fish in the net, Arthur helped her take it off the hook, and put it in a bucket filled with water. "It will make for a fine dinner for the three of us. You did good, Sea," Arthur said.

Chelsea's smile faded a moment. "*Sea?*"

"I thought I heard Henry calling you that. I liked the nickname." Arthur grabbed his rod and tossed his line back into the river. He started reeling it in slowly, flipping his rod into the air every so often. "Is that a nickname only Henry has for you?"

"Not really," Chelsea said. "You can call me Sea." She tossed her line into the river near his.

"So, you like it here?"

Chelsea reeled her line and tossed another. "It's not bad. It's definitely fun, catching your own dinner like this."

Arthur nodded. "Good."

They sat in silence, tossing their lines into the river. Arthur reeled his in. When there wasn't anything to say, he kept to himself. It wasn't an awkward silence, though. Chelsea was able to enjoy his presence, even if they weren't talking to each other. She took in the scenery. The beautiful line of trees that sat at the end of the blue river. The sprinkle of sunlight on the ripples made by the breeze. She could see the appeal of living out here.

Chelsea looked over at Arthur, tossing out another line. When he wasn't smiling, his wrinkled face looked almost sad.

Arthur reeled in his line and suddenly tossed his rod on the ground. Chelsea pretended not to notice.

"Did you hear me?" he said in a whisper.

"What's that?" Chelsea asked.

Arthur looked around, seemingly confused about where he was. "Nothing. Nothing." He patted his right jacket pocket and dug his hand inside it. He looked at Chelsea sternly. His jolly demeanour now vanished, and he looked almost menacing. "This isn't what I wanted." He removed his hand from his pocket with a grey pipe firmly in his grasp. He slipped his hand back in his pocket, taking out a bag of loose tobacco. He stuffed some in his pipe and took out a lighter.

"How'd you two do?"

Chelsea turned and saw Martha coming out from the woods. "I got one." She pointed at the bucket. "With Arthur's help of course."

Arthur puffed on his pipe, managing a smile. "It was all her, Martha. You should have seen it."

"Well, dinner will be better now that we have our protein," Martha said, beaming. She came close to Arthur, stretching out her arms, and wrapping them around his waist. As she did, she patted his sides. "Good job teaching her, dear."

"Teaching is easy with a good student."

Chelsea smiled. "Thanks, Arthur."

Martha looked around the river. "Getting closer to dinner time. How about we clean up here and I'll start a stew?" Before anyone could agree, Martha continued, "Chelsea, how about you bring the rods back to the barn? I'll help Arthur here. Go ahead."

Chelsea took the cue to leave. She gathered the rods

and made her way down the path towards the cabin. She was starting to get her bearings out here. As she left, she could feel Arthur's gaze burning the back of her head.

The man is not well, she reminded herself. Just like her grandmother, he would be lucid, present and then suddenly, he would be confused. She would tell Henry about it when he got back. She stopped on the path to look at her cell phone. It had already been over six hours since he left, but he hadn't texted or called her to let her know he was okay.

She sighed. Why can't men understand that we want a text to let us know they are safe? Chelsea thought to herself. At some point during the hike back to the truck and the several-hour drive to the city, he couldn't have messaged her? Something? Anything? He couldn't have left her a message letting her know somewhere along the way that he was okay.

A crack of what sounded like a tree branch made her stop in her tracks. The woods could be relentless too, Chelsea knew. There was the wolf that Arthur kept talking about. Henry shouldn't have hiked by himself to his truck. He could have at least brought a weapon with him like Martha recommended.

Chelsea spotted a large rabbit jumping through the wooded area where she heard the cracking sound. She smiled to herself. Arthur would love to catch you, Chelsea thought.

She continued walking towards the cabin. After several minutes she found herself in front of a large stump with the broken trunk on the ground. The massive tree had toppled a few other smaller ones around it when it fell.

Chelsea didn't remember this. It was a landmark that she would have recognized. She could feel her heart racing. How did she manage to get lost so close to the cabin?

She started wandering in different directions, trying to get her bearings again. She thought about yelling out for Martha or Arthur but didn't want to seem this incompetent. She finally spotted the edge of a roof and breathed a sigh of relief. Somehow, she'd managed to hike around the cabin.

Chelsea smiled as she walked the dirt path beside the

garden towards the barn. She noticed the shed was wide open. She also noticed for the first time that it had a deadbolt lock on the outside, finding that odd.

She went inside the barn and hung up the rods on the wall where Arthur kept them. She looked around the rotted-out building. She enjoyed the rustic feel of it. She almost felt the sense to paint a picture of this one, although scenery art wasn't what she enjoyed.

She enjoyed portraits more. In art school she knew she would be challenged, though, with taking on different types of paintings. Maybe she could use her in-laws' barn as inspiration for one some day.

She took in everything around her. The large traps on the wall. The shovels, racks and other long metal instruments leaning against one side. On a long counter beside her she saw several red stains leading towards a small tarp.

Chelsea knew she shouldn't look but couldn't help herself. She lifted the tarp, expecting to see the remains of a cut up chicken or some other animal. Instead, there was a tin box. A dark silhouette of a cowboy on a horse was on the front. Underneath the tin was a larger pool of dried blood staining the wood counter.

Curiosity got the better of her. She couldn't help herself now. She opened the tin and noticed a picture of Arthur holding the hand of a small child on top of a stack of other photos. Chelsea smiled at the happy look on Arthur's face.

Chelsea felt her phone buzz in her jean pocket. She took it out and saw it was a message from Neil.

"Hey, so you're still good for Tuesday at my place, right?"

Chelsea wrote back, "Definitely. Henry knows I'm seeing you that day."

She lowered her phone and moved the picture of Arthur to the side. She could feel what felt like a credit card in the box. Before she could grab it, her phone buzzed again.

"He's not coming over with you though, right?" Neil asked.

Chelsea sighed. That would probably not be a good idea, she thought. "No. Just us."

He wrote back quickly this time. "Good. We have to spend all night together on this until we figure it out. Could be a long time. Make sure he knows you're coming back late. You're mine that night. We need to figure out life in Toronto."

Chelsea rolled her eyes. "Yeah. We have a lot to think about," she wrote.

"Did you tell him about us living together?"

Chelsea rolled her eyes again. "Don't worry – I will."

"Maybe we don't have to. It could be our little Toronto secret. What happens in Toronto, stays in Toronto."

Chelsea shook her head. What the hell was he talking about? Instead of texting him back, she tried to call him, but the call dropped. She was about to leave the barn when she realized she'd left the tin box open on the counter. If Martha or Arthur saw that they would know she was snooping around. She ran back and closed the tin, putting the tarp over it again.

She quickly made her way into the garden and continued to try and call Neil. After a few dropped calls, one connected, but he didn't answer. She left a message. "Call me," she wrote sternly.

She took in a deep breath, typing to maintain herself. What the hell was Neil doing? Her phone buzzed again.

"We talked about this," Neil wrote. Another message popped up. "I thought you felt the same way?"

She couldn't believe what she was reading from her *supposed* friend. She felt sick with remorse. Chelsea wrote back in all capitals, "STOP TEXTING ME LIKE THIS. STOP!"

"What about Toronto?" Neil wrote.

"I have a lot to think about now," Chelsea wrote. She quickly turned off her phone and put it back into her pocket.

How could she have been so naive? Henry was right. She was gullible. Neil was a perv. How could he talk to her like that? He would joke around at times, sometimes she supposed it could come off as flirty, but Chelsea thought that wasn't his intention.

How could she be so *dumb*?

Martha and Arthur suddenly came out from a dirt path into the woods. Chelsea took in another deep breath and started walking towards them.

Arthur grimaced when he spotted her, raising a hand. "What the hell are you doing?" he shouted at her. "How many times do we have to tell you? Stop walking on the baby tomato plants!"

Chelsea saw in horror that she had smushed a small plant in her haste. She quickly made her way to a dirt path, tripping over a pile of loose soil. She looked up at Arthur. His face was one of rage. At that moment she felt afraid of him. Before, he'd looked so happy, timid even, but now she could see that side of him that Henry had told her about. Arthur was gentle until he wasn't. It was almost as if someone flicked a switch on his face from happy to furious.

CHAPTER SEVENTEEN

They call it a *quiet room* for a reason.

Chelsea sat on the kitchen table bench, pretending to be interested in the self-help book she'd grabbed from Henry's room. Martha and Arthur sat at opposite ends of the living room in their large fabric chairs. The fire in the pit blazed.

Every so often, Arthur would tend it, poking it, or adding more logs. Every so often, Martha would check her stew that was simmering on the stove. Chelsea sat on the bench, bored as hell.

She enjoyed reading, but it felt forced. Despite her boredom, and the feeling it would make her self-explode, it served a valuable purpose. She didn't have to talk to her in-laws. She wished they would read for the rest of the night until Henry came back.

Arthur had unloaded on her in the garden earlier. How could someone get so upset over a plant? Now he sat in his chair as if nothing had happened between them. After Chelsea felt she was finally bonding with one of her in-laws, Arthur showed his true colors.

She thought how good she would feel to see Henry again soon. Then it sunk in. Tomorrow was Sunday, her last day here. Now she could feel the boredom inside her turn to excitement.

Every so often, Chelsea would peek over her book to the front window, hoping to see Henry coming up the steps. She had turned her phone back on, hoping he would call or text her, but still nothing.

Chelsea messaged him several times.

Instead of Henry, Neil had texted several times, begging

for her to answer him. Chelsea read a few messages, rolling her eyes at each one.

She made up her mind that she would still go to Toronto, but Neil would be a less integral part of that adventure. They were not going to be living together, that much was certain. Thankfully, they hadn't given the landlord a deposit like Neil recommended they do before arriving in Toronto. Chelsea wanted to see the apartment., the neighborhood, before committing. Toronto was an even larger city than Calgary. She wanted to make sure it worked for her.

Chelsea looked out the window again, hoping to see Henry emerge from the woods. She only saw trees blowing, and the large garden.

Henry was right about Neil. He would be happy to know that when Chelsea told him. She would wait until they were well on their way from her in-laws. They had a long hike tomorrow and a few hours' car ride. Plenty of time for her to tell him *everything.*

"Something wrong?" Martha asked.

Chelsea looked up. "Sorry?"

"I'm not sure why you chose that self-help book. It must be completely boring. I have a bunch of books in my bedroom." Martha pointed down the hall. "Help yourself. It would be more exciting than one of Henry's books."

Arthur laughed. "Not sure she wants to read one of your dreadful romance novels, Martha."

Martha scoffed. "Well, spy action thrillers aren't likely her genre either." She looked at Chelsea. "I can't stand looking at you pretending to read any longer. Grab something you would actually enjoy."

Chelsea smiled and stood up. "Thanks, Martha." She went down the hall to the parents' room.

"I don't think it's locked," Arthur called out, "but if it is, Martha will come."

Please don't be locked, Chelsea thought. Thankfully it wasn't. She was taken back by how the bedroom was decorated.

The bedsheets were neatly tucked in. Chelsea was prepared to see a tidy room, though, given how Martha was.

The small, cozy room was painted in an off-white pink. Large plants surrounded it. Gold-colored picture frames hung on the wall. Many were pictures of Martha and Henry. One had Henry with his arm around Arthur.

The shelf had an enormous selection of novels to choose from. Arthur was right, Martha seemed to enjoy romance novels, all with different barrel-chested, half-naked models on the covers. It made Chelsea smile. For a woman like Martha who was so *Martha*, she was also a romantic apparently.

Arthur was right on another front; Chelsea didn't enjoy romance too much. She sifted through the shelves, looking at the titles. A few times she found one on the spine that interested her, but when she plucked it from the rest and saw the corny model on the cover, she changed her mind.

Of those that weren't romance, a few caught her attention. She was surprised to find *The Martian*. She read a few pages and decided to give it a try. She supposed it didn't really matter. Chelsea wasn't a fast reader. She wasn't the type to finish a book in a day, and she was leaving tomorrow, but she needed something to entertain her in the *quiet room.*

"I read that book." Chelsea was startled and turned to see Martha smiling at her. "I only read it one time, which is weird for me. Most of my stories I've read a few times over. I find when you take a look back at a story, after you've read it, you can enjoy it more, especially when you know what's coming. All the foreshadowing an author puts in, sometimes it goes right over your head when you read it the first time. I suppose that's why I like romance books so much." Martha plucked a book from the shelf and looked at the back cover. "They always have a good ending. The woman gets what she wants: her man. Things may look bad for the heroine but in the end, they live happily ever after. I couldn't read a story if I didn't know it would have a happy ending."

Chelsea smiled back. "I guess I'm the same." That was the

difference between real life and fiction. Sometimes the heroine doesn't get what they want. Sometimes terrible things happen. Martha wanted to be caught up in world of make-believe with her fiction.

Martha put a hand on her shoulder. "I want to apologize for Arthur. The way he raised his voice at you, it wasn't right."

Chelsea nodded. It's easy to forget how irritable someone can get when they are sick. "I know he's not *himself*."

"He's actually... better."

Chelsea lowered her head. She remembered what Henry said to her the other night. Despite how Arthur could appear, he was abusive to him and to Martha. She wouldn't dare bring it up though. "That's what Henry told me."

"Henry told you?" Martha said, surprised. "Well, I also want to let you know that I'm also sorry myself. In the garden. I didn't want to come off that way. Of course you are already married."

"Thanks for saying that, Martha," Chelsea said. "I love Henry, and I want us to get along, just like a mother and daughter would."

Martha's appearance changed. She almost seemed to sour instantly. Her face tightened, but she maintained her smile, making her expression more menacing.

"That's what I want too," she said. "Do you think you and Henry have that type of love?" She pointed at her books. "The type where you... complete each other, compliment each other's weaknesses."

"I do. It's been a hard year for me, despite meeting Henry. He has been there for me. He really is my *rock*."

"And how do you compliment him?"

Chelsea was taken back by the question. Suddenly the room felt smaller. She wished she could just leave, but Martha stood in her only path to the door.

"What I mean," Martha continued, "is how are you fulfilling what Henry needs? I think you should put back your choice of book and read one of mine. You will see."

"Thanks, Martha." Chelsea's face was blank. She tried not to show how upset she was becoming. One more night, she thought. None of this matters after. "I'm okay with the book I chose," Chelsea said politely.

"You don't know what *love* is," Martha blurted out.

"Martha, please, just stop."

"How could you know? Do you know what *I've* had to do in my life, for love? You wouldn't understand. You couldn't."

"Martha, I'm going to lie down in Henry's room for a little while. I don't feel so good."

Martha grabbed her shoulder. Chelsea could feel her strength.

"Let go of me," she said, but Martha tightened her grip. Chelsea shrugged her off forcefully. "I've been here with you and your husband this whole weekend, which feels like an eternity, and you haven't been nice to me once! Not once! You look down at me every chance you get." Chelsea desperately laughed. She was surprised at the words spewing form her lips. It was as if someone else had taken over her body. She had never been so upfront with someone before. Saying the words to Martha felt *powerful*. "I'm a good person. I'm an easy-going person. Henry loves me. He chose me to be his wife. Stop babying him! He doesn't need you anymore."

Martha took a step back from her. She raised her hand, and for a moment, Chelsea froze in fear of being struck.

Arthur's deep voice bellowed in the hall. "Martha! Come over here – *now!*"

Martha straightened and left the bedroom. Chelsea quickly left the room as well, going straight into Henry's and shutting the door behind her, wishing she could lock it.

CHAPTER EIGHTEEN

Chelsea lay on Henry's bed, staring off at the ceiling. She'd brought Martha's book into the room with her but had a hard time focusing on anything.

How could Martha act like *Martha*?

Chelsea tried to think of someone, anyone who frustrated her as much as her mother-in-law, but couldn't. Martha was queen in that regard.

Chelsea took out her phone. She called, but of course, Henry didn't answer. She wrote out a quick message.

"Please, if you get this, come soon. This is too much for me."

She looked at her phone, waiting to see any indication that Henry was going to respond, but nothing. She tossed it across the mattress with a sigh.

She thought of what she'd said to Martha. Chelsea had never spoken to someone in anger in that way before. Typically, when someone upset her, in her mind she would play out how she wished situations would go, but this time she'd done it in real time.

What would Martha have said, though, if Arthur hadn't *saved the day*. Martha had looked flustered to the point of rage. Chelsea imagined dodging a slap from Martha and closed fist striking her back. She smiled to herself.

Was she wrong to talk to her own mother-in-law in that way though? Chelsea certainly felt good in the moment. How would Henry feel, though, when she told him about everything that happened?

Her cell phone buzzed on the mattress.

"I parked the truck and I'm on my way to the cabin. Thank God. What a day," Henry wrote.

Chelsea smirked. "What a day indeed," she said to herself. She could almost jump up and cheer. Soon this nightmare would be over. Martha would back off a little once Henry came home. Chelsea would tell him everything that happened. He would surely be on her side.

That thought made her pause. Would he really take her side over his mother's? Would Henry make excuses for Martha – or even worse, side with her?

A knock on the door startled her. "Sea?" Arthur called out. "I put a bowl of stew outside the bedroom for you. You can eat in Henry's room. I don't care."

Chelsea stood up from the bed and opened the door. Arthur stood in the hallway, his bottom lip stiff, lowering his head.

"She's not here," Arthur said. "Martha, when she gets upset, which you can imagine how often that happens, she will go for long hikes. I'm sure she will be back in a while." He pointed at Henry's desk. "Martha hates it when I eat anywhere else besides the kitchen table, but what she doesn't know won't kill her." Arthur smiled, and Chelsea managed a smile back.

"Thanks," Chelsea bent over and picked up the stew.

"Crackers?" Arthur asked.

"I'm good, thank you. Henry just texted me - he will be back soon."

Arthur's smile vanished. "Good. Enjoy the stew." He limped down the hallway as Chelsea slowly closed the bedroom door.

She sat at the desk and ate. She was surprised how much she enjoyed the stew. Martha was a great cook. All the fresh ingredients added a level of flavor that Chelsea wasn't used to from her meals at home. Chelsea was the type to usually compliment the cook, but in this case, she would keep her comments to herself. The fewer words with Martha, the better.

When she finished her stew, she stood from the desk, grabbing the bowl and her phone, and left the bedroom. She walked down the hallway and saw Arthur reading his novel in his chair.

"There's more if you want some," Arthur said. "Plenty more, actually."

"I'm okay, thank you." Chelsea placed the bowl in the sink, putting her phone on the counter. She squirted some soap on the bowl and turned on the faucet.

"You don't have to clean up, Sea," Arthur said. "But since you are. try not to use too much water. I have to replace the jug under the sink. It hasn't rained the last few days so the rain barrel outside doesn't have too much to give us."

Chelsea nodded. She noticed the large pot on the stove boiling. She wondered what Arthur was making. He didn't seem the type to cook, and they had finished dinner already. She peeked inside the pot and saw a white bone turn around in the water.

"Bones," Arthur said, standing up. He made a loud groan when he did. He limped over to the stove. "Chicken bones. From the chicken we had the other day."

"What are you doing with them?"

"We try not to waste much out here. Everything can have a purpose, even chicken bones. I grind them up and use them in the soil for the garden. They have a lot of nutrients in them. The plants love it. Let me show you." Arthur grabbed a spoon on the side of the stove, tilting the side of the pot and lifted a bone out. As he did, the boiling hot water in the pot spilled over the side, and all over the counter. Some splashed onto Chelsea's arm, and she winced in pain, turning away.

"*Oh dear!*" Arthur shouted. "I'll get the first aid kit." He quickly made his way down the hallway.

Chelsea turned on the faucet and put her arm under cold water. She could feel pain on her left wrist where the boiling water had made contact. She felt a sigh of relief as the cold water washed over her burn.

She took a step and felt her feet warm. The water was all over the floor and counter. Chelsea lowered her head in defeat when she saw that her cell phone was another victim. It was drenched. She grabbed a towel hanging in front of the stove and quickly wiped it down. She pressed multiple buttons on her cell, but it wasn't turning on. Her screen remained dark.

"Fuck," Chelsea uttered.

Arthur limped back into the kitchen with a white box, taking out some of its supplies.

"I'm so sorry, Chelsea. Are you okay?"

Chelsea nodded. Arthur grabbed her arm and took a look. "I think it's just a first-degree wound. We can treat it, but we will keep an eye on it." Arthur took out his glasses from his shirt pocket and put them on, examining her wrist.

When Chelsea noticed, she took her arm back from him. "It really hurts."

"You must really hate us, eh?" Arthur said. "Burnt, broken now. I'm sorry for everything, everything." Arthur looked at the phone on the counter. "I don't think I can do too much about the phone, though."

"Do you have rice? We can put it in a bowl of rice and sometimes it will soak up the water, and if I'm lucky it will work."

"Bowl of rice. Who would have thought? Let me just bandage your arm first." He did so quickly. The pain still hurt but lessened as Arthur cared for it. "Did you do *that* to yourself?"

"What do you mean?"

Arthur lowered his head, and went to an upper cabinet, grabbing a bag of rice. He went into another cabinet for a bowl. "Your arm. Did you... *hurt* yourself?"

Chelsea put her arm to her chest, soothing it by rubbing gently. "I... don't want to talk about it."

"I didn't mean to hurt you."

"I'll be okay. I don't think my *phone* will be."

"Well, who needs them anyway? I'll clean up here."

Chelsea went back down the hallway towards Henry's

room. As she did, she heard a buzz. She looked back at her cell phone laying in the bowl of rice. Arthur had tossed a few rags on the floor and was using his feet to mop up the water. She heard the buzz again and realized it was coming from Martha's bedroom.

She quietly went inside and looked for the source of the sound. She opened the top dresser drawer. She dug her hand inside, trying not to make a noticeable mess, but could feel the vibrations. She felt an envelope and found what she was looking for underneath.

She took out a cell phone from her mother-in-law's underwear drawer and stared at it. She clicked the side of the phone and saw a new unread message from Henry.

"Not far away now. Will be back soon," it read.

Chelsea shook her head in disbelief. Martha had a *cell phone*, and was texting Henry this whole time? She quickly read a few messages.

Martha: Where are you? Are you okay?

Henry: I'm fine. I'm coming back now.

Martha: We need to talk about Chelsea.

Henry: Please, try and get along.

Martha: We need to talk when you get back.

Chelsea heard Arthur groan in pain from the kitchen. She quickly put the phone back into the dresser but felt something else inside. She cupped the object and took it out. When she opened her hand, she saw an emerald ring with a gold band, looped into a steel necklace. Several keys were also attached.

"Ah, fuck's sake," she heard Arthur shout.

Chelsea put the ring and keys back into the dresser. She closed the door quietly and opened Henry's door. She pretended as if she'd walked out of his room.

"Are you okay?" she shouted.

"I'm fine… fine," Arthur said. "Don't worry."

Chelsea smiled and closed the door, trying to catch her breath.

CHAPTER NINETEEN

Chelsea sat in Henry's room, not wanting to leave again.

She couldn't get her mind off the text messages she had read on Martha's phone. She was surprised she even had a cell, let alone knew how to text. She didn't come off like the type to have a phone to begin with.

She thought of the necklace with the keys and the ring. She remembered the ring specifically. She went to Henry's shelf and took out the pictures between the two books. She put back the one of Henry as a child and looked at the one of Carrie Sanders.

She hadn't really studied the photo of them together before. Now she had more than enough time to let it sink in.

The woman she assumed to be Carrie Sanders. The gold-banded emerald sat heavy on her left ring finger. The girl had a large smile on her face, with Henry matching her.

Henry was *engaged.*

He had never told Chelsea he was ever engaged. She knew Carrie meant a lot to him, but he didn't say he had proposed to her. Chelsea looked at the picture again, hoping in her daze that she'd mistaken which hand the ring was on. She breathed in deep, realizing she was right. The emerald ring was on Carrie Sanders' left ring finger.

Why didn't he say anything to her about Carrie? Henry was older, thirty-five. She expected him to have some type of baggage from his past when she met him. An ex-wife, kids even, but Henry told her he was a lifelong *bachelor.*

Now she couldn't wait for Henry to get back to the

cabin for multiple reasons. She wanted some damn answers. She wasn't sure if she would kiss him and thank him for saving her from his parents or interview him like a detective.

Who was this woman with the ring on her finger? Was it Carrie? Why did they break it off? The question burning inside her most though, why hadn't he told her?

Chelsea paced in the bedroom, the floorboards creaking as if it were part of an orchestra. She couldn't calm her mind. The only thing that stopped her in her tracks was the pain from her wrist. It was as if she could still feel her skin burning.

From inside the bedroom, she heard the front door open. She quietly peeked outside the bedroom door. She heard Arthur get off his chair.

"Henry!" he said loudly. He hugged his son. Chelsea saw Arthur speak in a low voice, pointing to his wrist.

"Is she okay?" Henry said loudly. He walked past his father and yelled, "Sea!" When he spotted Chelsea, he stopped and smiled. "Are you okay? Dad said your wrist was burnt."

"I'm okay," she said. "He patched me up."

Arthur walked up to them, Chelsea's phone in his hand. "Doesn't look like the rice worked," he said. "She's dead."

"May she rest in peace." Henry turned to Chelsea with a smirk, and it quickly vanished. "Wait, sorry. The pictures with your father were on there. Did you save them somewhere else besides your phone?"

Chelsea lowered her head. "I... didn't even think about that. No, I hadn't saved them."

Henry sighed. "Maybe we can bring it to a repair shop. With any luck there'll be something we can do."

"Let's go to bed," Chelsea said, defeated. "I'm beat, so I can only imagine how you're feeling." Plus, she wanted to play police officer with him in private.

"We got it sorted out. Crisis averted at work. It was worth the trip. Thanks, Chelsea." He turned to Arthur. "Night, Pops."

As they walked into his bedroom, Henry threw his backpack on the bed. "What a day."

Chelsea nodded, not truly caring about how her husband's day had gone. She sauntered to the bookshelf and took out the photograph of him and the woman.

"Who is she?" Chelsea asked sternly.

"I told you about Carrie," Henry answered.

"What's this?" Chelsea pointed a finger at the ring on Carrie's hand. When Henry didn't answer immediately, she brought the picture closer to his face. "You were *engaged?*"

"Chelsea," Henry said, breathing out deep, "it really has been a day. I can tell you everything tomorrow."

Chelsea shook her head. "I need to know, *now*, Henry. Why didn't you tell me?"

Henry bent over and took off his socks. "We were only engaged for a month. She took off on me, okay? I wish I knew what happened, but now that I met you, I couldn't care less where she is. I left for a business trip, and when I came back, she was gone. All her things, vanished, like she was never a part of my life. I look back at Carrie and me and realize she never wanted to be engaged to me. Why should I count that as being *formally* engaged? I was willing to fulfill my promise to her. I… wish I never asked her."

Chelsea sat on the bed beside him. "I didn't know any of that. You should still have told me. You should have told me more about your parents too, though. Why does your mom have the engagement ring?"

"What?" Henry asked. "It was a family heirloom, but she took off with it. How does Mom have it? Did she show you the ring? Was she trying to instigate something between you and me?"

"No, " Chelsea said, taking her time to answer. "I found it in her dresser."

"You snuck into my mom's room? What are you doing?"

"Not exactly. I heard buzzing in her room. Your mom has a phone?"

Henry laughed. "Of course. She lives out in the middle of nowhere. What happens if she needs help? I bought her the phone. I showed her how to use it. What's the big deal with that?"

Chelsea sighed. "Well, nothing, I guess. It's all... *weird.*"

Henry waved his head. "I'm not even gone for a whole day, and everything is going so bad."

"I'm sorry, Henry,' Chelsea said. "I wanted this weekend to work out well, but it didn't. I need to tell you what's been happening here." She took her time explaining the multiple run-ins with his mother. His father raising his voice at her. She finished her story with her reading her mother-in-law's text messages and how his mom had confronted her in her bedroom.

"She said that to you?" Henry said, amazed. "She said you aren't good enough for me? Who does she think she is? God, I hate this. Why can't she let me make my own fucking decisions without being on my back the whole time?"

Chelsea lowered her head. "I sort of told her to stop babying you."

Henry raised his head. "*What?* No, you *didn't.* How could all this happen in one day? How did everything deteriorate so quickly?"

They heard the front door of the cabin creak open, and Arthur greet Martha.

Henry took a deep breath. "I need to talk to her." He stood up.

Chelsea quickly stood beside him and grabbed his hand. "Can we not do that tonight? Maybe tomorrow, but just later. I've had *enough,* Henry. I can't handle much more."

Henry nodded. "Okay, fine. I'm just taking it all in. We can't keep talking about this. The walls are paper thin, as you know. We'll talk more on the way back to my truck tomorrow. We leave first thing in the morning."

Chelsea smiled. "I love you." She kissed him softly. "Oh, thank god you're back."

Several stern knocks on the door made them turn their heads away from each other. "Henry, are you back?" Martha called out.

Henry sighed. "Don't worry," he whispered to Chelsea. He stood up and opened the door. "Hey, Mom," he said in a low voice.

"I'm happy you're back," Martha said. She peered into the room at Chelsea and looked back at her son. "Can we talk?"

Henry sighed, but shook his head. "Tomorrow, Mom. It's been a long night. Let's talk tomorrow."

"But I need to tell you things," she said sternly.

"There's nothing that can't wait until tomorrow. Goodnight, Mom." Henry waved to her and closed his bedroom door slowly.

Henry slipped into the bedsheets and wrapped his hand under Chelsea's head. He kissed her softly. "First thing tomorrow, we'll leave. Right after I talk to Mom."

CHAPTER TWENTY

Martha

"Did you see what he did?" Martha said, stumbling up to Arthur. Arthur seemed indifferent to her, going back to reading an old magazine on fishing. Martha didn't repeat herself. Arthur had heard her. He was just being his typical difficult self. Dragging his feet along with everything they planned for.

Henry shut the door *on her*. Martha said she needed to talk to him, but he slowly closed the door on her. He may as well have slammed it in her face.

Did he forget *who* she was?

Arthur was the one who was *supposed* to have dementia, wasn't he?

At least that's how they planned it. Arthur was *difficult*, but nowhere near as demented as they claimed he was.

Martha was worried that the gun was missing, scared even. What would Arthur do if he had it on him? Did he have other plans that Martha didn't know about?

He didn't have the gun when he was fishing with Chelsea, that much Martha was certain. She'd almost patted him down like airport security when she met up with him at the river. She'd searched the home, looked anywhere she could imagine him hiding it, but she couldn't find the gun, or the tin box.

She thought about telling Henry about the gun. The gun was meant to be locked up for a reason, even if the reason was *made up*.

Martha changed her mind, though, when Henry shut the

door on her. Who could she even trust anymore?

Henry needed to know about the tension between her and Chelsea. He needed to hear her side of the story before his wife tainted his ears with *poison*. Instead, he'd closed her out. It was almost as if he'd stabbed her in the heart. Martha scowled at the thought.

She walked over to the kitchen, grabbing an apple she'd picked today in front of the pantry. She took out her Swiss army knife with the pink heart on it from a pocket on her dress. She took her time peeling the apple, thinking about Henry's face when he shut the door on her.

Henry chose Chelsea, over *me*, she thought. *Her over me.*

"I took care of her phone," Arthur whispered to her, lowering the magazine. "It's completely broken."

Martha smiled. At least she could still depend on him for some things. "Good. What about the shed? Is it ready?"

Arthur breathed in deep. "Not yet. I'll work on it tonight."

"It has to be ready *soon*."

"I know." Arthur lowered his eyes to the magazine. If Martha didn't know him, she would think what a cold-hearted bastard he was for not paying attention to her, but he had his poker tells. He was having a hard time with what was going to happen *next.*

Martha heard what sounded like laughter from Henry's room. It infuriated her more. Now they *laugh at me*? she thought. Who cares how old Martha feels. Only my dear *wife* matters to me now.

She took a bite of her apple, staring at Arthur intensely. "*Old man,*" she said to him playfully, "how about you take me to the bedroom? We can... *fool around* a little." She lifted her yellow dress, showing her upper thigh to him.

Arthur took in the view for a moment. "Just... *leave* me alone."

Martha laughed. "What? You don't want what you had last night?'"

Arthur folded the magazine and tossed it across the room

aggressively. He slammed his fist into the armrest of his chair. "Leave me alone, *woman. No more games.*"

Martha laughed again, turned and looked out the window. She smirked as she gazed into the garden. Arthur was right. *No more games.*

Tomorrow was the day they're supposed to leave. Martha smiled. The garden was full of people who thought they were going to be leaving as well.

Perfect, pretty Carrie Sanders thought she was going to *leave.* Now she was here forever, with the *rest of them.*

CHAPTER TWENTY-ONE

Chelsea tossed and turned for what felt like an eternity that night. As usual, Henry passed out, breathing heavily. She watched him lovingly.

She wondered what would it have been like if she'd met his family *before* they got married? She realized now Henry had his reasons to not have her meet his parents after all. This weekend would be enough to scare off most women.

Martha was on a different level of *motherhood*. Arthur – she couldn't figure out if she was afraid of him or enjoy his presence. Out of the two, she would rather be in his presence than Martha's.

Henry had managed to survive his parents his whole life though, and she would too. In the future she would *have to* visit them again, she knew. She would talk to Henry about not leaving her again, though. She would bring her own reading materials. She would avoid being alone with either of her in-laws.

She knew she would have to visit again, but it would be a long time from now that it would happen thanks to her starting school. With Chelsea gone for semesters, Henry would have more free time, and in turn might use some of that time to visit them. Martha would be happy about that at least.

Maybe art school was the answer to *everyone's* problems.

She felt the urge to relieve herself but did not want to leave the bedroom. When she couldn't resist any longer, she slipped out of bed and tried to make as little noise on the floor as possible. She opened the door with some fanfare, though.

A ringing sound like metal hitting metal made her stop in her tracks. She tried to look around the home for the source of the consistent thumping, but it appeared to be coming from outside.

Chelsea walked quietly down the hallway. When she passed the living room, she looked at Arthur's chair, but he wasn't there. From outside she heard a drilling sound. She peeked out into the dark from the front window. Light shone around the frame of the barn door.

Arthur opened the barn door and came into the garden. Chelsea quickly hid from the window. If he came into the cabin, she would pretend to be about to grab some water. Thankfully, Arthur he headed back into the barn. The light from the barn illuminated the hammer in his hand.

What was he doing so late at night? she wondered. The red light indicating the alarm was set was not on. Soon after Arthur passed out of sight, the clinking sound continued.

"Can't sleep?" Chelsea turned and saw Martha standing in the hallway. The darkness inside the home made her barely visible, except for her thick eyebrows and a smile on her face. Her long white nightgown flowed when she took a step towards her. Somehow, she had managed to not make a peep on the floorboards. Chelsea wondered if she floated down the hallway.

Chelsea nodded. "Just thirsty – and had to go to the bathroom." She looked out the front window and back at Martha. She thought about asking what Arthur was doing outside, but the less conversation between them, the better. Whatever Arthur was doing was not her concern anyway. In a few hours Henry and her would be leaving.

Martha's smile grew. "Well, you and Henry are leaving today. I hope you will come back and visit again."

"Of course," Chelsea said, managing a smile back.

"*When?*" Martha asked, tilting her head.

"I have to leave for school soon, so maybe after the

semester is over. I'll be back for the holidays. Maybe you and Arthur can come visit us in the city?"

"That would be lovely. Maybe we can garden again together today before you leave. I didn't tell you how helpful you were. You have really learned a lot out here."

Chelsea lowered her head. "We were planning on leaving early. Henry said he had to get back to the city to finish some more work."

"Henry – such a busy boy these days. He didn't tell me he was planning on leaving in the morning." Chelsea smiled thinly, unsure what to say. "Well," Martha continued after a brief moment of silence, "I'll fix you both a large breakfast before you leave. You will need some food in you before you hike back to his truck."

"Thank you, Martha," Chelsea said. "Well, goodnight."

"Goodnight," Martha repeated. Chelsea waited for her to leave, but she stood in the hallway, between her and Henry's room. Chelsea walked around her slowly.

"See you in the morning," Chelsea said.

Martha turned to her. "Chelsea." She waited for Chelsea to turn and acknowledge her before continuing. "Please remember to use *extra* sawdust after you use the bathroom. You forgot last time. I hope you come back, soon. You are always welcome in my home."

"Thank you, Martha, and I will." She went into the bathroom, and after using it, was generous with the sawdust as requested. She listened carefully until she heard Martha go back into her bedroom. The sound of whatever Arthur was doing outside continued.

When she was certain Martha was not going to come out of her bedroom, Chelsea made her way back to Henry's room. She slipped back into the covers and faced her husband. To her surprise he was staring back at her, wide awake.

"You, okay?" he asked. "I thought I heard you and Mom talking to each other in the hallway. Did she *upset* you?"

"No, she didn't. She *welcomed* me to come and visit

anytime."

Henry nodded. "Good," he whispered. "I wish... things had gone better this weekend."

Chelsea grabbed his hand under the covers. "Me too." Henry looked at the ceiling. Chelsea could tell he was upset. "I do have to say now that I've met your parents, I feel more connected to you. I know more about you and love you even more."

Henry smiled. "I love you for putting up with me after this. I was worried about how this would go, and it went far worse than I imagined. You sure you still want to be my *wife*?"

"How can I show you how badly I want to be your *wife*?" She wrapped her legs around his waist and pulled herself on top of him. The bed creaked when she did.

"What are you doing?" Henry said with a smirk.

"I'm going to make love to my husband... *quietly*."

CHAPTER TWENTY-TWO

The morning came and went by fast, to Chelsea's joy. They finished breakfast at the table, and Martha stayed true to her word; it was a feast. Chelsea was so stuffed she thought she would feel sick when hiking back to the truck. Even though it was their last meal together on the trip, surprisingly it was a quiet one.

Chelsea felt the tension but kept her comments to herself. When they did converse, they mostly talked about how beautiful the weather had been during their stay at the cabin. A highlight of the conversation was when Arthur told Henry how well Chelsea did at fishing.

"If it wasn't for her, we would have been vegetarians last night," he quipped. Henry laughed and Chelsea smiled. Martha seemed *indifferent*.

When everyone finished their meal, Martha reached out and grabbed Henry's arm. "Can we talk, *son*?"

Henry nodded. "Of course." He remained seated and waited for his mother to say something.

"I meant just us."

Henry looked at Chelsea and back at his mom. "Sure." The two of them left the table and went outside.

Chelsea stood up and started to gather some of the plates, bringing them to the kitchen sink.

Arthur waved at her to stop. "You don't have to," he said.

"What else are we going to be doing all day without you two around? Leave the mess. It gives Martha something to do."

Chelsea continued to clean up after breakfast. "It's no problem," she said. "It was a great meal. I feel like I need to help in some way."

Henry came back into the room and gave Chelsea a thumbs up. "Ready to go?" he asked.

Chelsea nodded. "I'll grab our backpacks from the bedroom." She left and got their things quickly.

When she returned to the main room, Henry was hugging his father and mother goodbye. "I'll be back soon," he promised.

"Well," Chelsea said, "it was great meeting you both." It was a lie, and she knew it, but didn't know what else to say.

"Thanks, dear," Martha said. She stood beside Arthur.

Chelsea wasn't sure if she should shake their hands or give them a hug. She should make some form of contact with them before leaving, she knew.

Instead of thinking about it more, she stretched out her arms and hugged Martha. "Thanks for the wonderful meals," Chelsea said.

"Hope to see you soon," Martha whispered in her ear.

Chelsea smiled at Arthur, but before she could reach out to embrace him, he put out his hand. Chelsea shook it.

"It was good to meet you, Sea," he said. His wrinkled face seemed indifferent in the moment. She thought it weird that Arthur and Martha were almost opposite in their typical demeanour when they were leaving.

She thought Martha would break down in tears, grasping her arms tightly around Henry's legs, begging him not to leave. Instead, she was seeing them out the door with a smile. Arthur appeared to be in more dismay than his wife. It could be that he was feeling unwell.

Henry and Chelsea walked down the dirt path through the garden. They both waved at Arthur and Martha one last time before leaving the property. Her in-laws waved back.

They hiked for several hours, and when they were getting closer to his truck, Chelsea couldn't help but ask.

"So," she said, "the one-on-one conversation with your mom, what did she say?"

Henry walked around a large tree, ducking under a branch. "It was relatively painless," he said. "She actually complimented you."

Chelsea laughed. "What? Really? What did she say?"

Henry looked back at her. "She said she thought you were a good person. She respects you. She said she can hopefully get along better with you next time you visit."

Chelsea couldn't believe what she was hearing. "Are you lying to me? I'm not as gullible as you think I am."

"Hey, I was just as taken back by what she said. Especially after what you told me the other night. I was expecting the worst. I told her I'd be back soon to check up on Dad after you leave. I need something to do when my heart is broken thinking about you being in *Toronto*." He said the city's name mockingly.

Chelsea changed the subject. "So, Carrie Sanders. You never heard from her again after she left you?"

Henry took a deep breath. "Yeah. *Nothing*. It was like I never existed in her life. Dropped me like a bad penny."

While Chelsea was obviously happy he wasn't with her, she couldn't understand what happened to their relationship to end that way.

"When did this happen?" she asked.

"I don't like talking about it," Henry said. He looked back at Chelsea and stopped walking. He took out a bottle of water from his backpack and took a sip. "Fine. I wanted her to meet my parents. We got engaged right at the cabin that night. I took her to this nice spot in the woods. There's this waterfall… Anyways, I proposed to her there. My mom and dad were in the woods hiding, and when she said 'yes' they came out clapping. It was nice."

"Did she get along better with your family?" Chelsea asked.

Henry rolled his eyes playfully. "This weekend was rough, but Carrie had her problems too with my mother, believe me. I thought though they liked each other when we left the cabin. Well, after a month of being engaged, like I told you last night, I had a business trip to Vancouver. She had moved into my apartment a few months before we got engaged. I was only gone a few days. When I came back to my apartment, all her stuff was gone. My place looked almost like it had before she moved in. She even took pictures of us together off our walls and around the house. It was like she never existed."

"I don't understand. You guys didn't fight or anything before she left? You can tell me, Henry."

He shook his head. "I wish I knew what it was. *Cold feet* maybe? I guess I'd rather have her do that to me then instead of running away at the altar." Henry looked at Chelsea and grabbed her hand. "It doesn't bother me anymore, though. She's history now, and I'm glad. I would have never met you and understand what *real love* means. Someone who can just run off on you like that didn't love me."

Chelsea kissed him. "I think you're stuck with me. I'm not leaving."

Henry smirked. "Well, you kind of are. *Toronto.*"

Chelsea hit him in the shoulder playfully. "That's not what I mean, and you know it. I would never leave *us*. Even if I'm physically further away from you, I'm still with you."

Henry smiled. "Good." He kissed her again. "So, I guess you and Neil have a lot to figure out on Tuesday."

Chelsea lowered her head. "Well, things are going to be *different* now."

Henry took another sip. "What does that mean?"

"Neil... isn't who I thought he was."

Henry furrowed his eyebrows. "What did he do?"

"He... came onto me. He was texting me things that suggested he thought we were *more than* friends."

Henry looked visibly upset. He shoved the water bottle in his backpack. "I knew it."

"You were right about him. I was *gullible* when it came to him, I guess. I gave him a reality check, though. We are nothing more than friends, and now I don't think we can be anything at all."

Henry nodded in satisfaction. "Good, but what does that mean for Toronto?"

"I'll have to figure things out for myself. I'm not sure what Neil is planning but that doesn't matter anymore."

"So, my gut sense tells me he's going to try again on you. I won't be there in Toronto to do anything about it."

Chelsea shook her head. "It doesn't matter what he wants. I'm not going to see him. You don't have to worry."

"I'm not sure what I'm more upset about though, the fact that I was right, or that he came onto you. What did he say to you?"

"It doesn't matter," Chelsea said. "I don't remember everything he said anyway. It was dumb."

"Too bad my dad broke your phone," Henry reminded her.

Chelsea grabbed his hand. *"Don't."*

Henry raised an eyebrow. "What?"

"Don't be upset about this. It doesn't matter. He doesn't matter to me. You do."

"Okay, I'll drop it. I just love you and worry about you being so far away."

Chelsea kissed him a few times. "I'll be okay. I survived a weekend with your parents. I'll handle Toronto by myself." Henry laughed.

They continued to hike through the woods. At one point Henry joked that he was lost, but Chelsea could see through his lame attempt at humor. She beamed when she spotted his truck in the empty parking lot.

Henry took out his key fob and hit the trunk release, swinging it open. He grabbed Chelsea's bag from her.

Chelsea immediately climbed into the passenger side of the truck, slamming the door a little too enthusiastically. When she sat in the leather seat, she could feel a wave of relief soothe her.

Henry shut the trunk but didn't immediately get inside. Chelsea looked outside the window at him, confused. He walked up to her door and knocked on the window, waving her to get out.

Chelsea opened the truck door. "What's wrong?'

Henry shook his head. "All four of them, *fuck*." He pointed at the bottom of the truck. Chelsea looked and saw both tires on the passenger side were completely flat.

CHAPTER TWENTY-THREE

Martha

Martha washed dishes, every so often looking out the window. Henry and Chelsea were taking their time getting back to the cabin. She paused while cleaning a pot.

What if Chelsea demanded they walk all the way to town? she thought. That would be impossible. They would be walking straight through the night.

Arthur limped over to her. "I'm sure they'll be back soon enough."

Martha ignored his comment. "I looked in the shed, and it's not *finished*." She glared at Arthur, waiting for him to explain himself, but he didn't. "That's not acceptable."

Arthur lowered his head. "I... don't think I can do this again."

Martha scowled. "*Weak!*" She dried the pot with a towel and put it in an under cabinet. "*Weak.* I'll finish it myself." She looked outside again. Out from behind the barn came Henry. Walking behind him she saw Chelsea with her long-sleeved white shirt on.

Martha looked at Arthur intensely. "Now is not the time to be stupid," she reminded him. Arthur nodded. They both went outside to greet them.

Arthur waved, managing a smile. "Missed us already," he

called out. Henry smiled, shaking his head. Chelsea folded her arms.

"Four flat tires," Henry said. "Must be a record. It must have been when I visited the construction site when I was dropping off my paperwork."

Arthur shook his head. "Only the one spare you have?"

Henry nodded. "Yep."

"That's too bad, dear," Martha said. "What will you do?"

Henry shrugged. "I called a mechanic, but they won't be able to come out to us for another day or two. I told them the tire size and they have to grab a few before they come."

"Well, you're welcome to stay as long as you need." She looked at Chelsea. Her daughter-in-law seemed defeated. She didn't smile. She lowered her head when Martha looked at her. Her *weakness* made Martha's smile grow. "Stay as long as you have to."

CHAPTER TWENTY-FOUR

When Chelsea was back inside the cabin, she made an excuse to be by herself right away.

"I'm not feeling well," she said to Henry, patting his chest. "Over eight hours of hiking drained me. My stomach hurts."

Henry looked at her sincerely. "Go lay down in our room. I'll bring you some water."

Martha put the back of her hand against Chelsea's forehead. "Well, you feel *fine*, but if you're going to... *regurgitate*, try and make it outside." Arthur stared at her with a look of concern.

Chelsea nodded and made her way down the hallway. She shut Henry's door behind her and lay in bed. It was barely past three. She would have to eventually leave the bedroom and be with them for dinner. She dreaded the idea.

No phone. No modern entertainment. Only more time with the Jameson family. It's what every girl dreamed of: more time with the in-laws.

She could picture Neil laughing at her when she told him. For a moment she forgot everything he had said to her. Maybe she *could* forgive him. Was there some way for them to be purely platonic friends? He had never shown that much interest in her until the other day.

The mechanic was coming tomorrow – at some point. She could suck it up another day, couldn't she? There were people on this earth having to deal with a lot more than Martha and Arthur Jameson. Being around her in-laws wasn't murder, after all.

Henry knocked on the door and opened it slowly. He had a large cup of water in one hand and a small bowl of stew in the other. "Mom had leftovers from last night. I'll eat with them but since you're not feeling well, just take your time and rest. Have some food if you want."

"Thanks," Chelsea said, sitting up in bed. She grabbed the bowl and cup and put it on the nightstand. "My stomach is in knots. I may just rest."

"That's okay," Henry said. "Yell out for me if you need anything. I'll check in on you soon." Henry leaned over and kissed her forehead.

"Thanks," Chelsea said, smiling. When Henry left the bedroom, her smile vanished quickly.

One more night, she told herself. For the love of God, one more night.

Chelsea finished the stew and lay in Henry's bed restlessly. She didn't want to leave the bed for fear that the floorboards would creak and give away that she was feeling better. Truth was she was feeling *fine*, physically at least. The only thing that would make her *regurgitate* was spending more time with Henry's family.

Chelsea thought about Toronto. Her life was about to take a huge turn. It was almost as if she was about to embark on an adventure.

She wondered if she would feel different when she was in school. It was not like her to go to another province and attend school. Painting was her dream. She worried about what would happen after school. How many successful artists did she know? The list was small, and full of artists who were famous and whose name everybody knew.

She could imagine Henry being happy that she'd completed her education to be a better painter, but disappointed that she had gone away from him, and was not more successful for it in the end. He wasn't the type to throw something like that in her face, but he would definitely think about it. Chelsea would think about it.

If that happened, Martha would likely not hold back her thoughts on Chelsea's adventure to Toronto. From how Martha talked, Chelsea could only imagine the things she held back telling people.

A stern knock on the door made Chelsea bring the covers up to her head, turning to her side. She instinctively knew it wasn't Henry.

She heard the bedroom door creak open, and she closed her eyes.

"Chelsea?" Martha said. Chelsea didn't move, but she could feel her presence at the end of the bed, staring at her. Martha walked across the bedroom. She felt a wind blow by her face, and knew Martha was standing over her. She heard the ring of china when Martha picked up the bowl and glass from the nightstand. Then she heard nothing at all. She knew Martha was still in the room somehow and was tempted to open her eyes. Instead, she pretended to be Sleeping Beauty.

After a few moments, she finally heard Martha make her way out. The bedroom door creaked as she closed it. For some reason, Chelsea worried that Martha was still in the room with her. It was as if she could still feel her presence. She waited for several minutes before opening her eyes, confirming she was the only one there.

She looked at the ceiling, taking in a deep breath. She closed her eyes and tried to force herself to sleep, at some point managing to do so. When she woke up it was dark, and Henry was beside her.

She quietly got out of bed. She spotted Henry's phone on the nightstand beside him and snuck around to look at it.

She clicked on the side of the phone and was happy to see that it was already ten at night. Somehow, she'd managed to stay in Henry's room the rest of the day, but was fully awake, and had to urinate badly.

Chelsea opened the bedroom door, noticing his parents'

was shut and no light came from down the hallway. She quietly used the washroom and was about to go back to bed when she started to hear the tinking of metal, and a drill. The red light above the door was not on, meaning the security system was not armed. She spotted light through the front window coming from the barn again.

What was Arthur doing there?

Chelsea knew she should go back to bed, but tonight the sounds coming from the barn felt more ominous. What was he doing?

She quietly made her way into the main room to look out the door, but then a creak in the living room made her jump in panic.

Arthur stood up from his chair. "Are you feeling better?" he asked.

Chelsea smiled thinly. "I got some good rest, thanks." She looked outside and heard the sound of a drill. "What is Martha doing out there?"

Arthur raised his hand, his eyebrows arched. "Don't go outside," he said sternly.

Chelsea took a step back. "I wasn't. I didn't mean to upset you."

Arthur pursed his lips and looked out the window and down the hallway. "This... isn't what I want. You need to know that. You need to be better with her."

Chelsea took another step backwards. "What do you mean?"

Arthur shook his head. "No. That's not going to work." He looked back up at Chelsea. "If I were you, I'd *run* from here."

The bedroom door creaked open and Henry stumbled down the hall, wiping the sleep from his eyes. "Everything okay?" Chelsea hugged him tightly, not letting go. "Sea," he said, "what's wrong?"

"I just want to go home," she said quietly.

Henry looked up at his father. "What did you say, Dad?"

"Nothing," Arthur said. "I'm just helping Martha. We

115

caught a rabbit in a trap; she's cleaning it out in the barn."

"At this time?" Henry said, raising his eyebrows. Chelsea maintained her grip.

"You know how your mother is," Arthur said.

Henry looked at his father intensely. "I sure do. We're going back to bed." Henry guided Chelsea back to the bedroom, closing the door.

"What did he say to you?" he asked.

"He scared me," she said. "I don't understand. He said I should run... away from the cabin."

Henry looked shocked. "He said that? Did he say why?" Chelsea shook her head. "I didn't notice – did he have anything in his hands? It was dark. I didn't see, I was so focused on you. He didn't have a weapon or anything, did he?"

Chelsea shook her head. "I don't think so." She remembered the story Henry told her about Arthur sitting in the dark with a gun in the living room.

"I should check with my mom," Henry said. "If this is how he is talking, we need to get him to a doctor right away. I can't let him take his time and come to the realization that he needs one when it's too late."

Henry started to open the bedroom door, but Chelsea shut it. "Don't go. Just stay with me, *please*."

Henry nodded. "My mom can handle herself, I'm sure. Just stay near me until we leave tomorrow. You can stay in our room until it's time to go back to the truck. I texted the mechanic and asked him to tell me when he puts on the new tires."

Chelsea smiled. For the second time in twenty-four hours, she felt like this nightmare was almost over.

CHAPTER TWENTY-FIVE

Chelsea pretended to sleep in the next day and took her time getting out of bed. Henry was up early. He said he would call the mechanic this morning for an update.

Henry opened the door quietly and came into the bedroom. "Good, you're awake. How are you feeling?"

"Better today," Chelsea said.

"Do you think you're ready to leave the *bedroom* today?" He smirked.

"Yeah. Any update from the mechanic?"

"He said he would call back when he was on his way to the truck. He has the tires but needs to make time to come out this way and will definitely make me pay an arm and a leg for the service." Henry looked out into the hallway. "Mom made breakfast, but it's a little *cold* now. Both my parents are out now. Mom went for a hike. Dad's fishing."

"Okay, thanks," Chelsea said.

Henry smiled. "I was helping Dad set up traps for the wolf early this morning. I'm beyond stinky from dragging them around. I'm taking a shower – want to join?"

Chelsea shook her head. "I'm actually really hungry."

Henry laughed. "Well, that's better than yesterday. Mom made a lot – as usual." Henry put his cell phone on the nightstand, grabbed some clothes from his dresser, and headed to the shower.

Chelsea took her time getting out of bed. She peeked outside the bedroom and when she felt comfortable that it was only her and Henry inside the cabin, she went into the kitchen. In a container were several pancakes with a side of bacon. A pot of maple syrup was beside it. Heavy carbs and sugar in the morning had a way of cheering any woman up.

She took out a plate from an upper cabinet and opened the container. She looked outside the front window at the barn and its surroundings. She couldn't spot Martha or Arthur anywhere.

What was Martha doing last night? What was Arthur doing the night before?

She opened the front door and made her way to the barn, carefully looking for her in-laws as she tracked up the dirt path. When she got to the barn door, she put her ear to it and listened carefully, but heard nothing. She opened it slowly.

When she went inside, part of the wall was covered in red paint splatters. When she got closer, she saw that it wasn't paint at all, but dried blood. The dark red spots stained the counter, walls behind it and the floor.

Chelsea put a hand to her mouth. Arthur said they caught a rabbit last night, but how could such a tiny creature produce this much blood? Chelsea thought.

Below the counter was the tarp she saw before. She remembered the tin box with the photos. One had Arthur in it with a little girl who couldn't have been older than two. She removed the tarp, and it was still there. The tin lid wasn't properly sealed. She removed it completely and the photo of Arthur was still there, but so was something else.

A silver handgun lay on top of the photos. Chelsea knew it wasn't there before. If it was, it wasn't on the top of the pile. Henry told her they locked up weapons because of Arthur's condition, so why was a gun in plain sight?

She picked up the gun carefully and placed it on the counter. She examined the photo of Arthur. The little girl had a bright smile beamed across her face, as did Arthur. Chelsea was completely lost as to who the little girl could be.

Chelsea looked down at the tin and saw what was underneath. She thought she'd felt a credit card when she was looking inside it before. She wished it was.

Her hand began to shake when she saw his picture on the government issued driver's license. Multiple licenses were inside the tin. Some had faces she recognized, while others she had never seen. One was someone she knew very well. Chelsea dropped Arthur's photo and attempted to pick up one of the IDs, but her body trembled and wouldn't let her.

She managed to grasp one and stared at it in disbelief.

"Henry McVoy". the ID read. Chelsea looked at the picture of Henry in disbelief. She dropped the card back in the tin and picked up another.

"Henry Shaw" now, but it was Henry's face that stared back at her.

Several other IDs were inside. None of them had the name "Henry Jameson" on them. All of them had the same picture of Henry on the front. She sifted through them all and found one that said "Caroline Sanders". She recognized the picture of the woman as Carrie, Henry's former fiancée. At the bottom of the pile was one that had Arthur's face on it.

Chelsea felt her heart beating out of her chest.

"If I were you, I'd run," Arthur had told her the night before. The day before he asked if she knew how to get to the highway. Chelsea felt like she had been struck by a bolt of lightning. Arthur was warning her.

The flattened tires on Henry's truck. Was it him who did it or his mother? Did Henry even call a mechanic? When Martha went on her epic hike the night before had she slashed the tires?

From inside the barn, she spotted movement beyond the garden. Martha was making her way to the dirt trail to the house. Chelsea ran out of the barn, back towards the house, before Martha could spot her. She made it inside the cabin quickly. Before closing the door, she looked back and let out a breath when she didn't see Martha.

She could still hear Henry inside the shower.

Chelsea went inside Henry's bedroom and shut the door quietly. His phone was still on the nightstand. She picked it up and with no password protection on his phone was able to open it to his home screen quickly. She opened the phone call record. No calls were made today.

She felt her heart sink. Henry never called a mechanic. Henry wasn't even *Henry*.

Chelsea began dialing 911, until she realized she was in the middle of nowhere with Henry and his parents. He'd lied to her about who he was. He'd lied about calling a mechanic. One of them cut the tires on the truck. She thought about the sounds coming from the barn late at night and the blood splattered everywhere inside it.

What did they have planned for her?

She cancelled her call to the police before completing it. Henry would see that she called 911. There would be no way of hiding that. The police would have no clue where his parents' cabin was. She would be stuck here with them until they could find her – if they could find her, if they even agreed to try.

She heard the shower stop running and panicked. She opened up a text message and put in Neil's number. Thankfully she remembered it.

"It's Chelsea. I'm texting you from Henry's phone. I need your help. This is urgent. Don't call this number but text me back right away!" She waited for him to respond. Henry would be back any moment. She tried not to think about what he would do if he caught her on his phone.

If Neil wrote back, she could ask him to help her, then delete the messages. Henry would never know she'd used his phone. Unless Neil responded after he was back. Chelsea panicked again.

His phone pinged. Chelsea breathed in deep, knowing Henry must have heard the sound. She quickly lowered the phone's volume to vibrate and opened the text message from Neil.

"What do you want? I've been trying to reach you for days, and now you come at me like this? Is this even you, Chelsea, or Henry messing with me?"

Chelsea tried to slow her breathing. She felt her heart was going to burst out of her chest.

"I don't know what is happening, but I'm scared of Henry. They won't let me leave. I need to escape and can't call 911. If you make it by Highway One, I can find a way to get there. This is not a joke. I'm scared, Neil, and I need your help."

Neil took only a moment to reply. "Okay. I'll leave now. What exit do you remember leaving last?"

Chelsea remembered the convenience store. The moody counter person and those kids. "The last place I remember was this convenience store off the highway before Banff National Park. Try and get there soon. Don't message me again, though, until I can get his phone and message you again. When I text you next, give me an update and I'll try and get out of here. Call the cops and let them know what's happening here."

Henry opened the bathroom door. Chelsea didn't have time to wait for Neil to reply. She quickly deleted his messages and put the phone back on the nightstand.

"Are you jealous?" Chelsea turned and saw Henry smiling at her, a towel wrapped around his waist. "*Phone* envy? When we get back to the city we'll drop by a mall or something and get another."

Chelsea managed a smile. "I wanted to check to see if the mechanic called."

"Did he?"

"I didn't have a chance to see but there weren't any messages on the screen."

Henry took off his towel, exposing himself to her. He dropped his clothes on the bed, taking his time getting dressed. Every now and then he would look at Chelsea with a smirk.

Chelsea felt like she was going to *regurgitate* for real now.

Who was her husband? Why did he have multiple IDs with different names? Why did he lie about the mechanic? What did he want from Chelsea?

She loved him. She felt so strongly that he was her soulmate. He'd been there for her in her despair over the past year.

All of it was a lie.

CHAPTER TWENTY-SIX

Chelsea left the bedroom as Henry changed. Her heartbeat continued to quicken. She couldn't imagine spending another moment near him. Flashes of their relationship sprung into her mind.

Their first date. The first time he said he loved her. The first time they made love. The day she moved into his apartment. All the memories flooded her mind with sorrow that none of it was with the man she thought he was.

Chelsea went into the living room and sat on Arthur's chair. She felt defeated, used, lied to. What was worse was she didn't understand what was happening. Why did Henry lie about who he was?

Martha opened the front door and took a few steps inside before stopping and looking at her with a scowl. Chelsea immediately noticed the black eye and swelling below her right eye. Martha lowered her head and continued to walk down the hall.

"I'm going to do some gardening," she said to Henry as he passed her.

Henry sauntered down the hallway towards Chelsea, brandishing a smile. "I talked to her this morning. I think you two are going to get along a lot better now. Tell me if she acts poorly again." Chelsea looked at her husband in fear and nodded. "I called the mechanic again in the bedroom. Was told he may not be able to come now for a few days."

"Oh," Chelsea said, rocking in the chair, "that's *bad news.*"

Henry looked at the container of breakfast on the counter. "You didn't eat anything," he said, turning to her.

Martha walked up the hallway with a new sundress on and a large hat on. She opened the front door and left the cabin without acknowledging either of them.

"It was too cold," Chelsea said. "Besides, I didn't feel like pancakes."

"Well, you need to eat something. It's going to be a long day for you." Henry opened the fridge and took his time looking inside, putting his phone on the counter. "Mom still has some bacon. Do you want to check the chicken coop for some eggs? I'll make you breakfast today." His smile widened, waiting for her to acknowledge his good deed.

Chelsea lowered her head, trying to catch her breath. She raised it again with a thin smile. "That... would be lovely. Thanks. I'll go check."

She stood up from the chair and looked outside at the barn. She remembered the bloody mess inside. She also knew the gun was there. Martha was walking through the garden towards the apple orchard on the opposite side of the barn.

Henry bent over and grabbed a pan inside a cabinet. Chelsea saw his cell phone on the counter and took a deep breath. She walked up beside Henry, wrapping her arm around him.

"Thank you for breakfast," she lied. "I love it when you cook for me." She reached around her back, grabbing his cell phone and slipping it inside her pocket.

"Well, I love you." He kissed her forehead. His kiss felt like acid burning her skin but she feigned a smile.

"I'll check the coop," she said. She walked out the front door, not looking back at him, and walked towards the barn. Martha was nearly out of sight on the other side of the garden. Chelsea quickened her pace.

She looked back at the cabin but couldn't see inside. All

she saw was the reflection of the sun on the window. Chelsea quickly entered the barn. She could hear the chickens in the coop on the other side clucking.

Chelsea immediately removed the tarp under the counter to grab the tin box, but it wasn't there now. She quickly scanned the room but couldn't find it anywhere. She had seen the gun and the box only a few minutes ago.

She took out Henry's phone.

"Have you called the police?" she wrote Neil. "Are you on your way?"

Immediately Neil wrote back. "Thank God you texted me. I thought about calling Henry's phone. The police didn't believe me. It's just me coming. I'm already on my way. Run until you hit the highway. I will find you. I'll be out all night until I do."

"Thank you! You were really there for me when I needed you. I need to go and find a way to leave here." Chelsea took a deep breath. How could she do this by herself? Martha was always watching. Arthur always seemed to surprise her when she least expected it. Henry was... she didn't know anything about him now.

The cell buzzed in her hand, and she opened his message. "I will do anything for the people I love."

Chelsea sighed. Neil was her only hope but why did he have to write that? She didn't have time to think about how to handle Neil when she saw him. She needed to get to him and worry about the rest later.

"Thanks!" she wrote. "Now I'm going to delete the messages, so Henry doesn't see. Don't write or call. I will find a way to leave and get to the highway." She deleted the messages and took one more look inside the barn for the tin box. She hated herself for not taking the gun with her when she could have.

She quickly went around the barn to the chicken coop. She shuffled past the chickens squawking at her and grabbed four eggs. She needed as much food inside her as she could get to make it through today.

She left the coop and looked out into the woods,

wondering which direction she needed to run. She remembered the way to the lot where his truck was parked. To get to the highway from there she only had to follow the road. The problem was, if she ran, Henry would look for her in that direction.

Chelsea looked towards the mountains furthest away from her. She remembered the formation was on the other side of the highway. That would be her best bet. If she continued toward the mountains, she would eventually find the highway, and Neil.

Chelsea took a few steps down the dirt path, then she slipped and nearly fell. An egg dropped and broke on the ground. Chelsea regained her balance and looked down at the shattered eggshell. She opened her mouth in horror when she realized what she'd tripped on.

An amputated finger lay on the dirt beside the broken egg. Chelsea bent to look at it. Ants climbed over the appendage. Maggots were at the bloody end of the finger. On the dirt path were clumps of damp mud that led into the garden.

Chelsea peeked around the barn at the cabin but still couldn't see anything inside. She followed the wet mud on the path to the garden until she spotted a shovel near the baby tomato plants, beside a mound of soil. Beyond the pile of dirt was a large hole, with a mass covered in plastic wrap in the middle. One edge of the plastic wrap hung open, flapping in the breeze.

She lowered her body into the hole, slowly tearing away the plastic wrap, immediately covering her mouth to stop herself from screaming. She couldn't help the tears coming from her eyes, and the squeals of terror escaping her lips.

Neil's lifeless eyes stared back at her. Dried blood ran down his head, and down the side of his face.

Chelsea took out Henry's phone and stared back at the cabin.

CHAPTER TWENTY-SEVEN

Henry opened the front door and called out to Chelsea, "Hey! What are you doing?"

Chelsea slipped the phone back into her pocket. "Picking some tomatoes for breakfast."

"Good idea. I was worried you got lost. I was about to send a search party for you."

Chelsea managed to smile back at him. Henry stood on the porch watching her. Chelsea looked into the woods and wondered if she could somehow outrun him. Even if she could – for how long? She picked two tomatoes close to her and slowly went back into the cabin. Henry held the door open for her as she stepped inside. Chelsea sat at the kitchen table and lowered her head. She placed the three eggs and two tomatoes on the table.

Henry picked up the eggs. "Only three? I could eat that by myself."

"My stomach is starting to bother me again," Chelsea said. She wasn't exactly lying. Her stomach had been in knots since finding Henry's, or whoever he was, multiple driver's licenses.

"Well, try and get some food in you. At some point, the mechanic will be at my truck and we'll have to hike all the way there together."

Chelsea took a deep breath, trying not to show how terrible that idea sounded to her. "Great."

Henry patted his jean pockets. "I can't figure out what I

did with my phone." He looked at the kitchen counter and at Chelsea with a smirk.

Chelsea could feel a tear forming in her eye. She quickly lowered her head and felt the phone in her pocket with her fingers.

Henry sat at the opposite side of the table. "You know, I've been wanting to tell you this. My parents don't care about…" He looked at her wrists. "They aren't the type to say anything to you. Maybe it's time you wear short sleeves, so you're not burning away out here. When wintertime comes, having long-sleeved shirts will definitely come in handy, though."

Chelsea looked at him, taking in a deep breath. "What do you mean?"

"Well, I was thinking, maybe Toronto isn't the best idea for you right now. We could stay. Who knows how long the mechanic will take to get to us? You could even miss your first semester." He waved his arms around. "Here. There's so little to worry about. You're going to love it here. Wait till you see— I'm about to ruin my surprise for you. I just can't contain myself. Staying here would be better though, for you."

Chelsea smiled, a fresh tear forming in her eye. "*Surprise?*"

Henry nodded. "You'll love it." He raised a finger. "I must have left the phone in our bedroom. Be right back." Henry got up and walked down the hallway.

Immediately he was inside, she felt Henry's phone buzz in her pants. Chelsea took it out discreetly.

"I'm on the highway now," the text from Neil read. "Find a way to go, now!" Chelsea looked down the hallway. She couldn't stop the tears from falling down her face.

Henry exited his bedroom and walked towards the kitchen. Chelsea quickly hid the cell in her pocket, even though she knew it was for nothing.

"What happened?" he asked her. He stood in front of her, wiping her tears. "Don't worry, Sea. *Everything* is going to be better now." Martha entered the cabin through the front door. She stared at Chelsea and Henry and started past them. "*Mom-*

wait." Martha stopped and looked back at Henry. He motioned her to join them at the table. "I'm about to tell her. Come sit with us."

Martha looked at Chelsea intensely as she walked back to the kitchen table and sat across from her, taking Henry's seat.

Henry sat beside Chelsea, grabbing her hand. He took a moment to look at his mom, and Chelsea, the smile on his face getting wider. "This... just feels so special. My two favourite ladies. Look at us, sitting together as a *happy* family. I'm feeling a lot of emotion right now. I don't know how to express it." He patted Chelsea's hand, staring at her intensely. "You really are going to love it here, with us. I know you will. You have to." He kissed her wrist. "I have something to show you. My *surprise*." He stopped and looked at Martha, raising an eyebrow. "Where's Dad?"

"He must still be fishing, dear," Martha said. "Should I run and get him?"

Henry scoffed. "Would take him a year to limp back here, and I can't contain myself any longer." He looked at Chelsea. "My parents have been working on a homecoming gift for you. You need to see it." Henry stood up from his chair, grabbing Chelsea and forcibly raising her off hers. "Don't be shy."

Chelsea wiped a tear from her eye. She looked at Henry, who gazed back at her coldly.

"What is it?" she asked in a whisper.

"Follow me," Henry demanded. "It's outside, in the shed."

CHAPTER TWENTY-EIGHT

Henry opened the front door, holding it for Martha and Chelsea. Martha walked outside.

"She's going to love it, Henry," she said to him, taking a moment to look at Chelsea.

"I have to thank you and Dad for all your hard work on this when I was away," Henry said. As they talked, Chelsea slipped the phone out of her pocket quickly and hid it behind a chair cushion in the living room. "Coming?" Henry asked her.

Chelsea smiled back and nodded. Henry put out his hand to her. Chelsea reluctantly reached out and held it. He guided her down the dirt path, with Martha several feet in front of them.

As they walked, Chelsea could feel her heart quicken with every step she took. Henry seemed happy as ever. Martha looked back at Chelsea and smiled. *Now* Chelsea was worried.

What were they planning for her? Should she run as fast as she could into the woods? Would she have a chance if she ran and hid?

They walked past the barn. Chelsea immediately let out a deep breath. She imagined them bringing her inside it, creating fresh paint of red blood from her body. They passed the chicken coop. Chelsea quickly glanced and saw Neil's amputated finger still laid in the dirt. They walked past the garden, and by Neil's shallow grave.

Finally, Martha stopped in front of the large shed. She

took out her keychain wrapped around her neck and opened the lock on the deadbolt. She glanced back at Chelsea. Her bruised face made her look puffier.

"I'm excited," Henry said, grabbing Chelsea's shoulders. "You're going to love me even more now."

Chelsea managed to give a thin smile back as Martha opened the door slowly. She went inside the dark shed, turning on a light inside.

A canvas was on an easel with the words 'Paint Me' on it. At the sides of the shed were a stack of other canvases. Multiple paint brushes and different small bottles of colored paint lined shelves that ran across the building.

Although the shed was black on the outside, the walls were painted white, giving it a more spacious look. She could still smell the last coat drying.

Henry laughed and pointed around the room. "I brought some of your paint supplies from our apartment here! A lot of it put in the drawers on the side there." He pointed at a large metal shelf. Displayed on the shelves were some of Chelsea's paintings. Some were completed that she was still trying to sell, while some she was still working on. "Organize this space as you like – it's all yours."

Henry looked at her, waiting for her to appreciate what he'd done. When Chelsea didn't say anything, his face soured a moment, then he smiled. "Now you have an art studio here," Henry said. "Who needs *Toronto*? You have everything you need right here. If you want any supplies, let me know. I can get you anything you need." Chelsea looked around the shed, trying to understand what was happening.

"You will have to thank my mom and dad," Henry said. 'When I was away, they did all of this. On top of that, they took care of the other *thing* I brought back with me." Henry looked out into the garden towards Neil's shallow grave. It was almost as if he wanted to throw what was happening in her face to see what she would say. Henry turned and looked back at Chelsea intensely. "You're not saying anything. Do you not like it? I put a lot of effort into planning this for you. I put a lot of time into planning this whole weekend, really."

Chelsea took a deep breath. "It's wonderful. Thank you," she said. She turned to Martha, who had a smirk on her face. "Thank you to you and Arthur as well."

Henry waved his hands around the shed. "Plenty of space. This is your *office*. You can do whatever you need to in here. Just ask mom or me to unlock it whenever you want. And- you're *welcome*." Henry leaned in and kissed Chelsea on the cheek.

Chelsea felt that sick feeling in her stomach again. "Well, I guess whenever I visit, this will be a beautiful space for me to work in. Thank you."

Henry looked at her and smiled. He turned to his mom. "What did I tell you? She still doesn't get it. We never have to leave here," Henry said with a laugh. "You don't have to leave for Toronto now. We have everything we need out here. We can be *together*, with none of the distractions that city life brings. Life out here is simpler. All we need out here is each other, and our *love*." Henry grabbed her hands firmly. "The Beatles – All You Need Is Love, right?"

Chelsea's bottom lip trembled. "What about our apartment?"

Henry shook his head. "I'll go back and move out the rest of our stuff that we need. We don't own the apartment. I pay the landlord with cash. When we aren't there anymore, let him try and find us out here to complain about it. No big deal."

Chelsea couldn't stop the tears from forming as he described her new life. They rolled down her face.

"But... the mechanic," Chelsea said, playing into his lie.

Henry waved her off. "They won't be able to find my truck. We're in the middle of nowhere. Even if I give them directions, they couldn't find us. *Nobody* can." He displayed a satisfied smile as he said it. Chelsea took in his words, and their meaning. She felt like a deer in the headlights watching the man she loved turn into a monster before her eyes.

How had she not seen him for what he was before? How

could she have been so *gullible*?

Henry swiped his hand across her face and looked at his mother. "Can you give us a minute?" Martha nodded and stepped outside the shed. When she was out of sight, he wrapped his arms around Chelsea, kissing her forehead. "This isn't an easy *transition* I know. Not everyone can handle it. I know that *you* can though. I have a good feeling about you. I always have."

Chelsea regained her composure. Wrapped tightly in his arms, she felt his strength. He had never hugged her this hard before. "Did Carrie Sanders handle it?"

Henry looked out into the garden. "No... she didn't. We weren't meant to be though. You and I are. That's why you're going to be *great*. I mean, I chose you for a reason. You're a good person."

"Are you going to... *kill me*?" Chelsea asked.

Henry laughed. "What? You're not understanding why I'm doing this. I want us to be *together*. I understand why you were tempted to go to Toronto, I do. Now we don't have to be separated. You can paint here. You don't need art school. Your pictures will look great in the cabin. I know you didn't really want to leave me to go to Toronto – with *Neil*." When he said her friend's name, his smile faded, and his hug tightened. "I wouldn't hurt you, especially if you're listening to all the rules."

"*Rules?*"

Henry scoffed. "It's already been a day for you. There will be plenty of time for me to go over everything. Just know that Arthur and Martha listen to the rules. That's why they are still here." Henry loosened his grip and let go of her. He tilted his head. "Well, sometimes people need reminders of the rules."

Chelsea looked behind Henry at the wall of the shed. Someone had painted over what looked like scratch marks on the wall. She immediately remembered the deadbolt on the shed door and lock. She turned back to Henry, who maintained his smile.

"You're going to do great out here. Not like the *rest*," he said.

Arthur entered the shed in a panic. "We caught it! We *caught* it!" he shouted. "The *wolf*! It's stuck in a trap by the falls. It's trying damn hard to get out. It's almost ripping out its paw in there."

"More *good news*." Henry peeked his head outside the shed at Martha. "Run and grab the gun from the house." Martha took off without a second word from her son. Henry looked at his father. "Well, let's go *kill* it. Will make a hell of head above the fireplace."

Chelsea started to cry again. Arthur looked at Henry, concerned. "I can stay with her."

Henry nodded. "Sure. By the time you get there the damn thing will have escaped." Martha was already on her way back from the cabin. In the distance, Chelsea could see the silver steel of the gun barrel gleaming as she ran. Henry patted Chelsea's arm. "Don't worry. Once I take care of this, it will be safer for you out here. You won't have to worry."

Henry left the shed and made his way down the dirt path to Martha. Arthur stepped outside and waved at the pair of them as they hurried into the brush.

Arthur turned to Chelsea. "That brought you almost an hour's head start," he whispered.

Chelsea wiped her tears. "What?"

Arthur pointed towards the back of the shed at the stack of canvases. "Behind there. I got your backpack ready for you. You need to run. Make it to the highway. Pray that a kind soul will stop and help. Don't *ever* come back here."

Chelsea thought about the tin box, with all the different drivers' licenses with other names on it, one belonging to Arthur. "Who are you *really*?"

Arthur let out a desperate laugh. "I was... like you. I've been here for over five years. Henry tricked me into coming out here, and I haven't been able to leave since." He shook his head. "I'm not his *father*. Thank God, I'm not his father."

Chelsea stepped towards the side of the shed, spilling some paint when she did. When she moved the stack of canvases, as Arthur promised, a backpack was there.

"Plenty of supplies, water, even a blanket. I tried to think of anything I could to help you get out of here, even if it took a few days."

"Come with me," Chelsea said.

Arthur let out another desperate laugh. "My leg. I wouldn't get very far. I'd slow us down. I've tried to run before, but I wasn't prepared like you are now."

Chelsea let in a deep breath. "Your leg, did he do that to you?"

"He did, after I tried to escape. I was stupid, I told that bitch Martha what I was planning, to help her too. She told him everything."

"*Martha?*"

Arthur waved his head. "I don't know who the hell that woman is, but she's not his *mother*." Henry looked out into the garden. "I know of at least three bodies out there. If we don't play his game, he *replaces* us. He tricks someone else into coming out here, to play a role in his twisted family fantasy. If they don't play along, that's it."

"You need to listen to his rules," Chelsea whispered.

"That's right. You don't play his game and pretend, you're going to be in trouble." He nodded towards the garden. "You'll join the rest of them. That's why I'm going to tell him that you struck me and ran. And speaking about that, you need to *leave* – now!"

Chelsea put the backpack on. Before she left the shed, she turned to Arthur one last time. "But *who* are you?"

"Fred, Fred Davies," he said with a smile. "Whatever happens to me, find my daughter, Eve. Tell her... I don't know. Tell her I love her." Arthur looked into the woods, then back at Chelsea. "Now get the hell out of here, Sea."

CHAPTER TWENTY-NINE

Chelsea wasn't sure how long she had been running for, but it was starting to wear her body down. Arthur, or Fred Davies, said she had only an hour or so's head start before Henry and Martha would figure out what happened.

Chelsea took no breaks, besides slowing down to catch her breath. As she hurried towards the mountain formation she'd noted before, she had one goal: find the highway. She could hide until a car came and try and flag it down.

She ran past a bush, scraping her arm. It was one of many bruises she was receiving while making her way to the highway.

Henry killed Neil, she thought to herself. He killed Carrie's Sanders. Fred said there were many more in the garden, buried along with her friend.

Chelsea ducked under a tree branch. She paused a moment, wondering if she was even still going in the right direction. She looked into the sky, trying to figure out what direction she was heading. She thought it would be easy to walk towards the mountain formation, but was worried she was already lost.

She thought of Henry. She imagined the last time she was intimate with him. Their bodies were one, and at the time, that was all she wanted. She wanted to feel connected with him. Now all she could feel was anger.

The sound of a howl interrupted her thoughts. She heard

the quick footsteps of something close by. She panicked inside, knowing Henry was close, until she realized the steps were too fast to be human. She turned and saw a large wolf running, jumping over a small bush towards her.

She looked around, and quickly attempted to climb a tree, but failed to get up it. The wolf was getting closer, and she ran to an adjacent tree with lower branches. She quickly climbed it as high as she could. The wolf stopped in front of the trunk, circling her. Chelsea attempted to climb onto a higher branch, but it was too flimsy. She stopped and looked down at the beast.

The wolf continued to circle the tree, and sat, looking up at her. It took a few moments for Chelsea to remember that wolves can't climb, and she immediately felt better. Then she looked down near the first tree she'd attempted to climb; her backpack was at the bottom of it.

Chelsea shook her head. She wanted to scream but feared Henry would hear. Chelsea cursed to herself, and at the wolf. She sat on the tree branch, leaning her body on the trunk.

The wolf at times would move around the area below her but was always in sight. Chelsea had no way of telling, but she knew she had been in the tree for some time.

She was *trapped.* The time spent running through the woods was catching up with her now. Her lips were dry.

It dawned on her in that moment that because Henry chose a cabin in the woods to bring his *prey* to, he was just as bad as the *wolf.* Just like the animal, Henry would keep her in the woods for as long as he could until one day getting bored with her – and adding her to the garden.

Chelsea felt lightheaded. Her thirst became unbearable as time went on. She closed her eyes and it made her feel better.

Every so often, Chelsea opened them again, but the wolf was still there. After a while, she felt her nausea and light-headedness increase. Closing her eyes to everything around her helped. She started opening her eyes less and less, until at some point she passed out completely, with the last image in her mind being Henry smiling at her.

CHAPTER THIRTY

Chelsea opened her eyes and saw the ceiling of the cabin and Henry in the corner of his bedroom, looking at her with concern.

"I was so worried," he said, getting closer. He took a damp warm cloth and pressed it against her face.

Chelsea moved around Henry's bed but couldn't shift her arms. She turned her head and saw rope wrapped around her wrist, tied to the bed side. She attempted to wiggle her arms out but couldn't.

"Hey," Henry said. "Take it easy. You're lucky we found you. Dad said you ran off on him. Hit him even, which makes sense. He's weak. He wouldn't be able to catch you. What didn't make sense, though, was he told me you ran off one way, but the footprints of red paint told me you went a different way." Henry laughed. "Now I'm not bad at tracking, but even a small child could have figured out where you went."

Chelsea raised her head and looked around Henry's room. Martha stood in the corner with a glass of water in her hand. Henry waved her over, taking it.

"You were severely dehydrated," he said. He tilted the cup and Chelsea tried to take some water in but coughed out most of it.

"Arthur?" Chelsea said between coughs. "Where is he?"

"Fine, he's *fine*," Henry said. "Don't worry about him. You just get better. What were you doing in the tree?"

Chelsea lowered her head. "A wolf chased me there."

Henry scoffed. "Imagine the irony of that. Dad said he

caught the wolf in a trap, but meanwhile it was out chasing you around the woods. You could imagine my surprise when there was no wolf in the trap by the Falls where dad said he caught it. Dad was also surprised by that when I *told* him."

"Did you... hurt him?"

Henry smiled but ignored her question. He turned to Martha and gave her the glass. "Can you get some more water, *Mother*? We need to talk, so take your time coming back." Martha nodded and left the room without a word. Henry waited to hear her footsteps go down the hall before turning back to Chelsea with a sympathetic look. "I know why you ran. I should have done a better job at telling you. Be more honest about your *situation*, about us. You will come to terms with it though. I know you will. You have to." Henry grabbed her wrist and squeezed. "For me, you have to for me."

Chelsea lowered her head. She couldn't meet her lover's gaze without tears forming. "Why are you doing this?"

Henry tilted her head back to him. "You like *him*, right?" Chelsea didn't answer, not sure what he was asking. "Arthur Jameson? He is an improvement. You should have seen my last few fathers. My biological father, Arthur, was a ruthless man. Beat me, my mother. He tore me down in life. Never once did he raise me with respect!" Henry lifted a finger in front of Chelsea's face and lowered it. "Now, he's *better*. Not perfect, but *better*. I like my father now. Martha. I like her better now too. The Martha I had at birth would join my father in beating me. She encouraged it at times. She's *better* now, too. Not perfect though. My parents made my life hell! Now we're a *happy* family. And now that I have you in my life, it's even better. Soon we can give my parents *grandchildren*. We can live *together*. It will be perfect. And if it's not, I will find someone else to help make it perfect." Henry smiled.

Chelsea lowered her head. "Don't hurt me."

Henry nodded. "The ropes, that's just a *precaution*." He yelled for Martha, who came into the room with another glass of water. Henry took the glass and put it on the nightstand. "Can

I have your knife?" he asked. Martha took her Swiss army knife out of her pocket and handed it to him. Henry opened it and began slicing the rope until it broke. He reached across the bed, gliding his body across Chelsea's, taking a moment to kiss her on the lips. He cut the rope on the other side off as well.

Henry handed the knife back to Martha and gestured for her to leave the bedroom again. "Trust is what makes a marriage work. I read that. We need to trust each other. I trusted you when I left the box in the barn with the gun. You could have killed me with it but didn't. I mean, it didn't have any bullets in it, but you didn't know that." Henry shook his head. "You running, this was my mistake, not yours. I didn't explain the *expectations* to you, the rules. If you knew them, you wouldn't have broken them. I should have done a better job, and for that, *I'm sorry*."

"What do you want me to do?" Chelsea asked, bringing her hand to her chest.

Henry grabbed her hands and held them tightly. "I want you to be *you*. I want you to keep loving me, as my *wife*. But a few ground rules. Martha is my mother. Arthur is my father. Whatever you may have heard, that's how you refer to them."

"Who am I?" she asked.

Henry laughed. "Chelsea Jameson, of course, my wife. At night, the system locks us inside. There are sensors on the windows. When the system is off, you can leave the cabin. Don't please don't leave like yesterday *again*. If I can't trust you, well, ask Arthur." He smiled again.

Chelsea lowered her head, trying to hold back her tears. "Is there anything else?"

Henry looked at her intensely. "Always love me, like your husband." Henry patted Chelsea's hands. "You know, they say you choose who you want to marry in life, and I've done well on that front. I want you to know you were the only one I've ever *married*. A few times I thought I was going to get married, but they didn't work out. I learned that it was better for us to get married first before I bring you here. Then you could love me for who I am. They say you choose who you're going to marry. I realized you could also choose your family as well."

CHAPTER THIRTY-ONE

Martha

Get her another glass of water, Martha. Get her a damp cloth, Martha.

How can he *still* care for her after what she did? She tried to run from him, but he couldn't care less.

The one time Martha tried to run from him, he beat her senseless. Her hearing on her right side still hadn't fully recovered from the strikes to her head.

Now, of course, he trusts me, with good reason. I made sure everything runs smoothly for Henry.

Meanwhile, Chelsea runs. What does she get? A glass of water. A caring kiss. Untying her from the bed!

Martha waited outside Henry's room. Soon Henry would call out to her with another request for his *dear* Chelsea. Martha would do what she was told, though, with little resistance. She knew better than to speak back to him.

Her master plan had fallen *flat*. For the last few weeks, she had been priming Arthur with ideas that Henry was going to make them bury more bodies in the garden. She'd seen how horrified Arthur was at burying Carrie's Sanders. He wept the entire time. Arthur was able to keep his composure when he buried the previous *Arthur* before him. The previous father of Henry couldn't keep it together. He attacked Martha with a knife. Thankfully, Henry saved her and put a bullet in his head.

Soon after, he was replaced with the current *Arthur.* Frederick Davies.

When the *current* Arthur tried to escape, Henry showed him little remorse. He injured his leg with a shovel. He wasn't able to walk for over two months, although Martha knew he was malingering, playing up to the idea that he couldn't bear weight to not be around Henry. What Arthur didn't know was that by not killing him, Henry was being sympathetic to him. Usually, escaping would lead to *replacement.*

Martha touched her swollen eye. It had been some time since Henry struck her like this. Martha knew she deserved it. She'd tried to get into Henry's head about Chelsea. She wouldn't make it out here, she knew. She tried to reason with him, explain it to him. His emotions were high, and she tried to talk to him at the wrong time.

He didn't care much for that. Martha put the cold compress on her eye and felt a sigh of relief from it.

Martha encouraged Arthur to help her escape. She'd told him fake stories that Henry wasn't happy with his current wife. He begged her to tell him that she would be okay out here, that she didn't need to be replaced. He would keep asking her if she "told him yet". Martha smiled. She had played Arthur well. When Martha told him that she couldn't reason with Henry about keeping Chelsea, he took it upon himself to help her escape. He thought he was being sneaky filling up a backpack with food and other supplies. He reminded her of herself when she was younger, escaping her parents. He'd done exactly what Martha wanted him to. Chelsea did exactly what she was supposed to do: escape.

Martha's plan had fallen apart with Henry.

Martha sighed to herself. The careful planning, the manipulating of Arthur, all of it was for *nothing* now. Henry forgave Chelsea immediately. No black eye or broken leg. Only care and attention.

Martha knew better than to say something to him,

though. She was already on thin ice. She touched her eye with the rag again. She had been in this place before, but always came out on top. She survived those times, and she would continue to.

She was a *survivor*. Arthur, Chelsea, none of them knew what she had to endure to *live*. She would do *anything*. Henry would see her value again. Henry would come to see *her* again, not these other *little girls*.

Henry would *love* her again.

"Martha!" Henry yelled from inside his room, undoubtedly with another request for his ailing wife.

"Coming!" she yelled back. She fixed her sundress before entering the room.

Martha was a survivor. She would outlive all of them. All she had to do was wait for another opportunity to arise, then Henry would see that Chelsea needed to be *replaced*.

CHAPTER THIRTY-TWO

Chelsea was allowed to lay in Henry's room for some time uninterrupted, mostly resting. The feelings of nausea had left as well as the slight headache she had since waking up in the cabin. She dreaded when Henry or Martha would check in on her.

She hadn't heard from Arthur since being back in the cabin. She didn't hear his voice outside the room, or his limping footsteps down the hall. Henry, or whoever he was, didn't say what had happened to him.

Henry had disabled him for life when he attempted to escape the cabin in the past. What would he do now that he'd helped her run away?

There was a possibility Henry accepted Arthur's story that he was shoved by Chelsea when she escaped, but she doubted it. When Henry saw no wolf in the trap, that would have been hard to explain. A knock on the bedroom door startled her. She turned to her side and closed her eyes.

The door slowly creaked open, causing her heartbeat to race. "Sea?" She turned and saw Arthur leaning against the doorframe. The entire left side of his face was swollen. He had a crutch made from long, thick branches tied together with rope. He limped into the room.

Chelsea covered her mouth in horror. "What has he done to you?"

Arthur put a finger to his lips. "I'll recover," he whispered.

"He didn't break anything that wasn't already broken. You need to come out of the bedroom now. It's dinner time."

Chelsea laid her head on her pillow, closing her eyes, wishing she would wake up from this nightmare. "I can't."

"Sea, look at me." Chelsea turned to Arthur. "You need to get into your *role* here. You can't do this much longer, *believe* me. Please, come to dinner with us."

Chelsea looked at him, concerned. Most of his face was black and blue. When he spoke, he winced in pain. Arthur had put himself at risk for her. Now she was back where she started, and it was all for nothing.

Arthur reached his hand out to her. "*Please*," he repeated.

Chelsea got out of bed, slowly, and held his hand. "I'm *sorry*," she whispered.

Arthur lowered his head. "Me too. For everything they made me do. Now, let's go. They are waiting."

Arthur slowly made his way down the hallway towards the kitchen table, with Chelsea slowly behind him.

Henry sat at the end of the table. He smiled when he saw Chelsea. He gestured for her to sit beside him, and she reluctantly did. Arthur, even slower than usual, made his way and sat on the other side of the table. Martha stood over the stove, pouring stew into bowls. She placed one in front of everyone at the table and sat in an empty chair.

Chelsea noticed that her face was noticeably less swollen now. Her bruising had gone down substantially. Arthur looked a lot worse now. Both her *in-laws* looked like they had been through a battle.

Henry looked at everyone at the table, taking his time staring at each. Arthur coughed, wiping his mouth, and winced in pain. "I can't imagine my life without you all," Henry said. "I'm grateful. Not everyone has a *beautiful* family like me." He looked at Chelsea. "Soon, Chelsea and I hope to have *children* of our own. We can add more love into this home." Chelsea could feel her stomach turn as he spoke for them. Henry lowered his head. "Let us give grace before this meal."

"Grace," the three of them said in unison.

"*Grace*," Chelsea whispered.

Henry smiled. "Looks *great*, Mom."

"Thank you, dear," Martha replied curtly. "It's just vegetable soup today. Arthur didn't catch any fish." She looked at her *husband* intently as if to shame him before continuing. "I picked everything out from the garden today, though."

The three of them began to eat, but Chelsea stared into her bowl. A cut up tomato floated at the top. She thought of Neil's body decomposing in the garden, and immediately stood up, purging what little she had in her stomach on the table and floor.

"I said *outside!*" Martha yelled.

Henry put a hand on Chelsea's shoulder. "She needs more liquids. She must still be dehydrated."

"I made her soup," Martha said with a scowl. "I made her soup so she could get more *liquids* in her."

Chelsea closed her eyes and wrapped her arms around Henry. For a brief moment, he felt the way he did *before* she found out who he really was.

"I need to lay down again," Chelsea whispered.

"Of *course* she does," Martha said, raising her hand. "She always needs to be in Henry's room."

Henry looked at her with a raised eyebrow. "*Enough*," he said. Martha listened.

Henry helped Chelsea back into their bedroom. She lay on the bed, and Henry covered her with sheets. "I hope you feel better *soon*," he said. "I'll be back with some water." He left the room and Chelsea turned to her side and closed her eyes. All she wanted to do was lie in this bed forever, until she realized it would be night soon, and he would be lying beside her.

She imagined sitting at the kitchen table with Henry and her in-laws. Chelsea had a bruised lip and dark bruises around her neck. Martha had a fresh black eye, and Arthur was still recovering from his injuries.

Chelsea knew it was only a matter of time before she herself felt the wrath of her husband.

She thought of what Arthur said. You need to *pretend*. She thought of the garden, and of Carrie Sanders, who was buried somewhere in it.

Henry came back into the room and put a glass of water on the nightstand. He turned to leave. "I'll come back soon, to *check* in on you."

"Wait," Chelsea said, sitting up in bed. She took a long sip of water before standing. "I'm feeling *better* now." She managed a smile as fake as the ones Henry had been giving her. "Thank you, my love, for taking good care of me." She wrapped her arms around his waist and kissed him on the lips. Chelsea fought back thinking about the monster she was married to and tried to picture what he used to be. She managed to kiss him several times. "You always take care of me."

Henry smiled. "I'm glad you appreciate me for that. Martha is cleaning up in the kitchen, but I will bring you your soup to the bedroom to eat."

Chelsea shook her head. "No, I want to eat with you, and our *family*."

CHAPTER THIRTY-THREE

Chelsea continued to act the way Henry *wanted* for the rest of the day. They sat in the quiet room, reading together as a family, each with their own books. Chelsea continued to read *The Martian*. Arthur, another action story, reading slower than usual. Martha sat in her chair, brandishing a smile every now and then as she read her romance. Henry was more than excited when he found his cell phone stuffed behind a couch cushion.

Henry stood up and told them it was time to lock up for the night. Martha shut the front door firmly. Arthur took his time getting out of his chair, wincing in pain with every movement.

Henry watched him intensely. "Goodnight, *Father*. Feel better in the morning." He turned to Martha and said the same. Henry took out his cell phone and tapped its screen. Above the front door, the light turned red. Martha and Arthur walked down the hall towards their bedroom.

Henry pointed at the camera in the living room. "It's motion-sensored, with audio capacity as well. So, it will start to record visuals and audio if it senses you when the system is armed." He pointed at the windows. "Don't open them either at night. The system is pretty loud when it gets set off. Just so you know, but I *trust* you now." Henry reached out to Chelsea. "Let's go to bed." Chelsea smiled again, amazed at how well she was *acting*, and took his hand.

When they were inside the bedroom, Chelsea sat on the

bed. Henry closed the door. He stood in front of her, taking off his clothes, as Chelsea watched, trying not to scream, but managed a playful smile. When he was down to his briefs, he sat beside her. He threw her hair to one side and began kissing her neck, the way she *used* to like.

She put out a hand on his bare chest. "I'm... well, it's *that time*, honey."

Henry raised his eyebrows. "Oh, I see." He removed his hands from her.

Chelsea kissed him softly, pretending to enjoy his lips. "That's probably why my stomach has been bothering me a lot. I'm really tired too."

Henry nodded. "Yeah, *long day*. Of course."

Chelsea lay down on the bed, turning to her side. Henry spooned her, wrapping his arm around her. Chelsea breathed in deep, waiting for him to remove it, but he didn't.

Chelsea looked outside the window into the dark forest surrounding the cabin.

How long can I keep *pretending* for? Arthur has been here for years. He's alive, but for what *purpose*? Who knows how long Martha has been here for. She's bought fully into her role in Henry's life.

Henry took a deep breath and nestled his body closer to hers. She could feel his warm breath on the back of her neck. She wanted to scream and run out of the room, but closed her eyes and calmed her breathing.

Her arm was extended out on the bed, her long sleeve in the palm of her hand. Chelsea pulled back her sleeve and looked at the marks on her wrists.

What *purpose* did her life have, when she was trapped in Henry's make-believe one?

CHAPTER THIRTY-FOUR

After breakfast, Arthur decided to lay in bed. He wasn't looking well.

Martha came out of the bedroom, wearing a white sundress with short sleeves and a matching hat. The sundress was laced around the sleeves. She looked quite stunning, Chelsea thought. Unless you saw the personality wearing the outfit, she would pass for a beautiful older woman.

Chelsea was sitting at the kitchen table with Henry having coffee when Martha walked up to her.

"Would you like to join me in gardening today?" she asked.

Chelsea had other *plans.* "No thanks, Martha."

"What else are you planning on doing?" she asked with a smirk. "You live here now, and you need to *contribute.*"

Chelsea smirked back. "I *will* be." Chelsea gestured towards the walls full of animal heads, fish and horns. "I want to fill these walls. Make it livelier here." She looked at Henry with a smile. "I wanted to paint today in my new workshop, is that okay?"

Henry kissed her. "Of course," he said while looking at Martha. "I would love for you to make this house more of a home with your art." Martha scoffed to herself and left through the front door in a hurry.

"This is a change for everyone," Henry said. "A good

change, but my mom will get used to it. Don't worry."

Chelsea nodded. She stood and washed her mug in the sink, placing it on a rack to dry beside other pots and bowls and a large kitchen knife. She took a moment before she turned to him again.

"I love you," Chelsea said. "*Goodbye.*"

Henry smiled. "I can't wait to see what you'll paint for me."

"No peeking until I'm done," Chelsea said in a low voice. She left before he could say another word. As she walked through the garden, towards the shed, she saw Martha gazing at her while she picked some fruit and placed it into her basket.

Chelsea used the tip of her finger to poke the knife further up her sleeve, placing her arm at her side, concealing the bulge of it.

"Martha," she called out to her, "can you please open the shed."

Martha slowly made her way over to the shed. She took the necklace from around her neck and unlocked it, gesturing for Chelsea to enter.

"You know," Martha said sternly, "Carrie Sanders didn't like this shed very much. She *especially* hated it when Henry would lock her inside for days. One time a *whole* week." Chelsea raised her hand to her mouth and wanted to cry but didn't give her the satisfaction. "Henry, he's been very kind to you," Martha continued, "but that will be coming to an end someday soon. That pretty face of yours will be *like* mine." She rubbed her bruised skin. "Don't try anything else funny around here," she said, pointing a finger into Chelsea's shirt. "I will know, and I'm *watching.*"

Chelsea nodded. Martha, even though she might not have been Henry's real mother, had his best intentions at heart. She was not like Arthur.

Martha smiled. There was something in that moment that got to Chelsea's core. It made her disgusted with Martha. Her mother-in-law was trying to frighten her. Why?

It was Henry. It was all about *Henry* for her. She wanted to be the number one person in his life.

Chelsea had thought Martha was just an overbearing mother, but that was obviously not the case. Chelsea was a *threat* to her being the top woman in the cabin. It struck Chelsea as if she had been hit by lightning.

Martha turned and started to walk away, but Chelsea called out to her. "Martha!" Martha stopped and turned. Chelsea walked up to her, keeping the sleeve with the knife concealed at her side. "Henry *loves* me, not you."

Martha's mouth gaped. "What did you say?"

"You heard me,' Chelsea continued. "He loves me. He *married* me. Look at your face. Look at Arthur. I ran away and *look* at me. Nothing. He didn't *touch* me. In fact, he loves me more right now than ever. Just wait until I tell him that you *struck* me."

"What!" Martha growled. "I didn't touch you."

"That's not what I'll tell him. Who will he believe? Me or you. What do you think?"

"*Me,*" Martha said softly. "I've always been there for him. You're the pretty *new thing* that has his attention, for now."

Chelsea smirked and waved her head. "We took a *sacred* vow. We're married. You're nothing to him, compared to me. Don't believe me?" Chelsea jabbed her finger into Martha's white dress. "Let's try it. Let's both go to him right now and see what happens. What do you think?"

Martha took a few steps backwards. "You're *different* now. You see what made me the way I am. You think you can *win*, over me?" Martha took another step back. "You may think you have the upper hand, but you don't. This was a big mistake you made."

Before Chelsea could say another word, Martha turned and swiftly left towards the garden. Chelsea stepped inside the shed. She went up to the canvas on the easel. She turned and picked up a brush, and looked at the paint, wondering what her last painting would be.

It was a mistake talking to Martha in that way, Chelsea knew, but none of that *mattered.* She slid the kitchen knife out from her sleeve, placing it below the canvas on the easel. After her painting was done, she wouldn't have to care about anything *anymore*.

One last cut was all she needed.

She stared at the canvas, thinking inspiration would spring out of her, but all she could think about was how she wanted it all to end. She was *trapped*. No matter what she did, her fate would be the same as her friend Neil. That was inevitable.

The question was, would it be Henry and Martha that put her out of her misery or would she have to take action for herself?

What would be Arthur's fate?

He put himself on the line for her. If Chelsea completed what she wanted to do, how much longer would Henry keep his *father*? She felt he was already close to being *replaced*.

Chelsea slid the knife back into her sleeve and left the shed. She didn't see Martha or Henry, and quietly made her way into the barn. She went past the fishing rods and traps, and made her way to the tarp under the counter, praying for a miracle. When she lifted it, the tin box with the gun, of course, wasn't there.

Chelsea cursed to herself, and quieted when she heard people talking outside. Through the decaying panels of wood that made up the barn, she peeked through a small hole and saw Martha and Henry talking.

At first, they spoke in soft voices, until Martha raised hers. "He needs to go, and so does she."

Henry shook his head and said something she couldn't hear. She put her ear to the hole, hoping to hear better, but it didn't seem to help.

"When she's asleep, help me bring him to the garden," Henry said.

CHAPTER THIRTY-FIVE

Martha

Martha brought her basket of fruit into the cabin. Henry sat in the living room, staring at his phone. She looked at him, waiting for him to acknowledge her existence. Instead, whatever he was looking at on his phone was more important.

Chelsea was more *important,* too.

Her words at the shed had cut deep into her soul. For a moment, Martha felt like she was that little girl being cornered by her father in the kitchen. She had thought she would never feel that way again, until Chelsea came into her life. Until *Henry* brought her into their lives.

Before she came, things had been *better* for the most part. Now Henry acted as if she wasn't even there.

Martha went down the hallway. She opened her bedroom door but looked at Henry's door. She quietly opened it and went into his room. On the dresser was a picture of them.

It had been a long time since they took this photo, and they both looked so good, and in love. This was when she first met *Henry,* or Henry McVoy as he was called at that time. He was a troubled boy. His parents were even worse than Martha's, Henry told her.

Martha loved him from the first time she met him. Martha smiled to herself. How long had she been calling herself Martha? She had almost forgotten who she really was. Rachel Bertrand.

After escaping her parents, she lived in a shelter in

Calgary for mostly runaways for years. The staff knew many of the younger people who lived there had come from terrible homes. Even after she turned eighteen, they let Martha live there a few years before saying she needed to move out. Even when the time came for her to pack her bags and leave, they helped her. The shelter gave her a job. She worked mostly with the youth, helping those who came in who were just like her. She had empathy for the young runaways especially.

She met many young people who would come and eventually leave the shelter. Many she knew didn't do well after they left. Some, she heard, *killed* themselves. Others ended up in prison. Martha liked to think she helped the young broken ones who came into the shelter a *purpose*. She talked to them. She listened to them. She was a shoulder to lean on.

Martha knew that it wasn't her fault that terrible things happened to them after they left the shelter, but that didn't mean that it didn't hurt.

The broken *stay* that way. Nothing could make them feel whole again after they ran from their homes.

Even though working at the shelter helped, Martha never felt whole. Helping others gave her a purpose, though. It made her feel like she was meant to go through the terrible things she had endured. She was *meant* to help other broken things as best she could.

She had worked at the shelter for years until one night, a new boy came, Henry McVoy. He was handsome. Young. Even though she was much older, she felt giddy being around the seventeen-year-old.

She connected in a way she hadn't with any other boy or girl who came to the shelter. She told him things about her life she hadn't told anyone. She told him everything except what happened with her father that night.

Then Henry told her the truth of what happened to *his* parents, and why he ran away. He had put a deer rifle to his mother's head first. When his father, startled, jumped out of bed, Henry took care of him next. He left, hitchhiked across the country, before coming to Calgary. After meeting Martha, he said he didn't want to go any further west.

Soon after, he turned eighteen. The shelter was forcing him to leave. Rachel could still feel the pain she had when she was forced by the shelter to give him the news he was being kicked out. She decided then and there that he would stay with her at her apartment.

He agreed. They became intimate soon after. She never thought she would fall for a boy over a decade her junior, but with Henry, it was easy.

One night, she told him the truth about what she did to her father. Henry understood. He had done it himself. It was either her or her father. She made the right decision, just as Henry had.

They fell even more in love. Henry started to work under a fake name. He had made a few connections with some people at the shelter who knew how to counterfeit identification. He was able to work as a security guard at a company under the name Henry Jameson.

He made solid connections at work, climbing the corporate ladder. More and more, he was away from the apartment. Rachel felt like he was losing track of who he was. What was the point of being with someone when they were never home?

Rachel made the mistake of telling him one night how upset she was. He accused her of trying to leave him. She insisted that it wasn't the case, but the truth was she had thought about it. It didn't matter to Henry. That was the first time he struck her.

The next night he surprised her with an emerald promise ring. He told her he was sorry for what happened. He didn't want to hurt her. He loved her and one day would marry her. When things were better at work, they would be engaged, and have a large wedding. They would invite the whole shelter. Anybody Rachel wanted to come could be there. He said he was working on a surprise for her. It would be something that would change their lives *forever.*

Then he took her to the cabin in the forest. She couldn't imagine how Henry had been able to build a home. Ingenuity and cheap labor from migrants on the street. They had worked day and night and completed the log home in a few months. Henry dropped them off in the parking lot and would hike with them to the spot he wanted to build. They weren't allowed to leave until the cabin was finished, only going to get more materials.

Martha loved the cabin. Henry said she should get rid of her apartment and move in with him there. It would only be the two of them, in the middle of nowhere, nothing but their love to warm their home. They would live off the land. Make their own garden. They would never rely on anyone but each other for their life out here. Someday, they could have children of their own.

Martha agreed, and a few years of being with Henry was more than she could have ever asked for. She loved her life with every year that passed. Henry, though, was becoming more distant again. He would leave the cabin for longer stretches to work.

He wanted a child from Rachel, but every month would bring more despair.

For years she tried to give him a baby, but couldn't.

Henry would be frustrated every time her period came. He started to try less and less to have one with her.

Rachel said she could go to a doctor in the city. He could see one too. Maybe there was something he could do to help so she could become pregnant.

Henry didn't like that. More years went by, and she remained without child. Rachel was now in her late forties. Henry resented her age. He blamed her for not being able to give him a baby.

"Family means *everything*," he would say.

After a weekend gone from the cabin, he returned with an older man in his late fifties. He was someone he'd met through work at a function. Jonathan Melroy was his name, at first. They had been fishing together in the city sometimes during breaks from work.

Henry had invited him to stay at the cabin with them for a weekend, but when the weekend was over, Henry told him he wasn't able to leave. Jonathan fought back, but Henry continued to hurt him until he *obeyed*. He started calling him his *father*, and named him Arthur, which was his real dad's name. He was only to answer to Arthur. If he didn't listen or called himself Jonathan, Henry would hurt him.

Henry was h*appy* again. He had a loving girlfriend, and his new *father*. Soon after, he brought an older woman to the cabin. She was Jonathan's real wife, it turned out. He tricked her into coming to the cabin under the guise of finding Jonathan. She was happy when she found her husband alive, but then found out the truth. She wasn't going to leave the cabin now.

Now her name was *Martha*, which was Henry's mother's name. *Arthur* was her husband. They were the parents of Henry. Rachel, his loving girlfriend. Henry had everything he wanted, except for a child.

At first, Rachel was scared for these strangers in their home. She didn't want Henry to hurt them. Just as she did in the shelter, she tried to help them make the cabin their new home. She would help them as best she could by helping them play their *roles* better.

Soon, though, they conspired behind Henry and Rachel's backs to escape. When they tried, Henry shot and killed Jonathan. Rachel helped Henry bury him in the garden.

Martha agreed she would never try to leave again and Henry, loving as he was with his *mother*, agreed to let her stay. Soon a new *Arthur* came to the cabin. Martha didn't keep her word and broke the rules. She didn't want to play Henry's game any further. Rachel had to help Henry bury her body in the garden as well soon after.

Every so often, someone would need to be *replaced*. Every year the garden would get bigger, and every so often a new body would be buried in it. Still she was not able to give him a child.

Soon, Fred Davies came to the cabin with Henry. He fitted in well and took to his role as *Arthur* better than any of the others. Henry was happy until his *Martha,* who'd played his mother for a few years, fell *sick.* She tried to explain to Henry that she had cancer but had thought she was in recession. Henry wouldn't allow her to leave and see a doctor. She died in her sleep next to Arthur some time after.

The next day, Arthur and Rachel buried Martha.

As they buried her, Henry dug a fresh hole in the garden nearby. When they finished burying Martha, Henry confronted Rachel in the garden, alone. He had a gun in his hand.

"I love you," he said, "but I need a family. I need a *child.* I want to be a father. Someday I'll be old and sick, like Martha. I need my children. You can't give me that." Henry raised the gun to Rachel's head, and she closed her eyes waiting for him to pull the trigger, but he didn't.

He stood there with the gun in his hand, pointing it at her, tears streaming down his face. "I *love* you," he repeated.

"This doesn't have to be the end for us," Rachel said. "You need a *Martha.* You need someone who loves you for who you are. I will never stop loving you and only want the best."

"You only want the best for me," he said.

"Of course I do." Tears streamed down her face as she said the words. "You need me by your side. Let me be *Martha.*"

Henry lowered the gun and grabbed her hand, taking the emerald ring off her finger. "You know we will never be the same, though, right? This is it. If I don't think you can handle it, I can't have you being something you're not." Rachel nodded. Agreeing so that she could live. All these years later, she still wished she'd let him shoot her dead that night.

Henry reluctantly agreed not to kill her, and for her to become the new Martha. He was also true to his word and never touched her as a girlfriend ever again. The three of them lived in the cabin for some time together.

Soon, he brought Carrie's Sanders to the cabin. She was beautiful, young. Martha, as she was now called, hated her from the moment she met her. Henry proposed to her that day. He put Martha's emerald ring on Carrie's finger. Martha felt her lip tremble. Her hands shook. She wanted to scream.

Carrie was supposed to stay a weekend, and soon found out, like all the others, that she wouldn't be leaving.

She didn't take that too well. Martha might have provoked her into breaking a few of Henry's rules. She might have lied here and there about things Carrie said to get him to see that she wasn't *right* for him.

One night, he finally recognized it for himself. He put her in the shed, attempting to force her to love him. Martha told him you couldn't *force* love, it had to be natural. He didn't listen for months. Finally, one night, after months of poor Carrie Sanders being in the shed, he understood.

She wasn't right for him. After he killed her, he kept her in the shed. He kept her body locked inside, to visit her when he was at the cabin. He came less and less to visit, though. It was as if he was in mourning for the woman he loved. It destroyed Martha every time she watched him visit her in the shed.

Martha hoped that now that Carrie was gone, she could talk to Henry about them. Instead, one night he came home and told them about Chelsea. He'd spotted her while working at the hospital on a small contract. He watched her. Took pictures of her. Eventually he found a way to inject himself in her life.

As soon as Henry told Martha, she knew things were going to change again. Whatever Henry wanted, he would get, she knew.

After their marriage, he told them they would be coming soon. He instructed them to get rid of Carrie's body and to clean the shed thoroughly.

As always, Martha and Arthur did what was told to them.

When Martha opened the door and met Chelsea for the first time, she hated her immediately, just as she did Carrie. She was *different*, though. Chelsea was less combative than Carrie. She loved Henry more than Carrie.

Now Martha found herself in the present. Chelsea was

Henry's new love. He'd made it clear that he would put Chelsea above Martha.

Martha put the picture frame of her and Henry back on the dresser. She took out the Swiss army knife from a dress pocket on her apron. She smiled, looking at the pink heart on it. Henry had given it to her the first year they lived at the cabin together. Every so often she would take it out to remind herself of her *worth* in Henry's life.

How could Henry be so stupid over this *little girl*? Did youth and good looks make men utterly dumb to what mattered in life?

Martha slipped the knife into her apron pocket and went into the hallway to confront Henry, only he wasn't inside. She spotted him walking through the garden and hurried to catch up.

She was nearly out of breath when she reached him. "Henry!" she called out. He stopped and turned to her. It was as if he'd somehow rolled his eyes at her before she had even said what she wanted.

"What is it?" he asked sternly, stopping near the barn.

"Where are you going?" she asked.

Henry let out a deep breath. "I wanted to see how Chelsea's painting was coming along. Get a *sneak peek*."

"You know I put us above everything, you know that, right?"

Henry shook his head. "I don't know what to do with you anymore."

Martha lowered her head. "I only have us in mind, but I know you're not seeing things clearly. We know Arthur helped Chelsea attempt to escape the cabin. Today, he tried again," she lied.

"What?" Henry said with a laugh. "No way/ He learned his lesson – hard. I'll have to find a way to make the cabin wheelchair-accessible for him after what I did. He's been in his room all day."

"Not at breakfast time. This morning, when you were

taking out the washroom buckets to the compost. I went into the bedroom and left them at the kitchen table."

"Why did you do that?" Henry said, raising an eyebrow. "Did you really think that was a good idea?"

"I wanted to see what they would say," she said.

Henry folded his arms. "Well, what did they talk about?"

"*Escaping*, what do you think," Martha said raising her hand. "She said she was just *pretending* to love you." In truth, Martha had that conversation with everyone who Henry brought to the cabin. It was best to play the role Henry assigned to you. If you didn't, you paid the price. She had told Fred Davies that when he first came to the cabin the same.

"Pretending?" he said, confused. "She just said that to him."

"She saw what you did to Arthur. She saw my bruised face. She called you *crazy*. She said when you start working again that she will plan her escape. She's going to call the cops and tell them everything that's happened out here."

"What did Arthur say?"

Martha lowered her head. "He was encouraging her. He told her his *real name*. "

Henry scoffed. "He did that?"

Martha nodded. "How many times have you told that old man? How many chances will you give Chelsea? He needs to go, and so does she."

Henry paused before speaking. ""When she's asleep, help me bring him to the garden," he said. "Let's go inside the cabin. I want to hear Arthur say this himself. You better not be lying, Martha. I'm already at my limit with you too. He goes either way. I was a fool for thinking I could trust him. Nothing happens to Chelsea."

Martha nodded.

"Say it," he demanded.

"Nothing happens to Chelsea."

CHAPTER THIRTY-SIX

Chelsea heard Martha and Henry talk. She understood Arthur didn't have much time left. She gathered what she needed from the barn and after confirming Martha and Henry were inside the cabin, quietly made her way back to the shed to set up.

She took her brush and sporadically spread paint on the canvas. She took red and blue, dunked her brush in the paint, and madly ripped her arms across her torso, splashing paint across the canvas. She herself was covered in different paint colors. When she was done, she took one look at her painting and took it off the easel, laying it purposefully on the ground, making sure to be extra careful.

She stood up and, satisfied that everything was right, she hurried down the path to the cabin. She tried to get herself into her *loving wife* character that Henry was getting used to before opening the door.

When she entered the cabin, Arthur sat at the table with Henry and Martha standing over him. The other side of Arthur's face had fresh bruises. Chelsea looked at Martha and knew that whatever was happening, her sweet *mother-in-law* was the cause of this scene.

Chelsea plastered a smile on her face, ignoring what was going on between the three of them. "Henry," she said. "I need to show you my painting."

Henry looked back at her solemnly. "Can it wait? I think the four of us need to talk."

Chelsea scoffed. "I made you something, in the studio you

spent days creating for me. Don't you care to see what I've made you?"

Martha rolled her eyes. "Henry, talk to her."

Henry looked at Martha and back at Chelsea. "I'd love to see the painting you made for me. Why don't you bring it inside. We can hang it up."

"You're going to love it, but it's still wet. I just want you to see what I've been working on all day for you." Chelsea went across the room and grabbed Henry's hand. "Come, let's go. You're *taking* forever!"

"You're excited?" Henry said, surprised.

"I love my painting, my work area, and you." She kissed him, tugging harder on his hand.

"Fine, fine," Henry said with a laugh.

Martha reached out and grabbed their hands. "We need to talk about what happened," she said sternly. "The painting can wait."

Chelsea took her other hand and removed Martha's grip forcefully. "*Mom*, stop. I want to show my *husband* something I made for him. I don't need your permission to do that, do I?"

Martha took a step back, not knowing what to say.

Henry smiled at her. "Hey, she's the *boss*, Mom. What can I say? Stay with Arthur, we'll be back."

Chelsea tugged on his hand and guided him out the front door. They strolled down the dirt path, holding hands. For a brief moment, it felt like she had the old *Henry* back.

When they were further away from the cabin, Henry let go of her hand, and stopped. "So, Martha told me something," he said softly. "I have to ask you about it."

Chelsea scoffed. "What did *she* say now?"

"She said Arthur told you his *real name*. Is that true?"

Chelsea took a deep breath in. How could she have known that? she thought. He had told her his name before she ran, and Martha was nowhere near them. None of it mattered anymore, though.

Chelsea nodded. "He did. The night I ran away. I didn't

know the proper ways then, though. You hadn't explained the rules to me yet. I made him tell me. I saw the different IDs in a tin box in the barn."

Henry nodded back. "So it wasn't *this* morning that he told you?"

Chelsea laughed. "No. When could he have? He can barely walk, or talk for that matter."

Henry nodded again. "Martha said you spoke to him about *leaving*, about not loving me."

"What?" Chelsea exclaimed. "When would I have had a chance to talk to him about that? He went to his bedroom after breakfast." Chelsea knew Martha was plying Henry with lies. Arthur and her never talked about escaping after the night she ran. Martha thought she would get the upper hand on Henry, playing on half-truths. She would take a page out of her dear mother-in-law's book on how to *play* Henry. "Martha was the one who *threatened* me."

"She threatened you?" Henry said, folding his arms.

"When she opened the shed for me today," Chelsea said. "She told me Carrie Sanders was buried in the garden, and that she would make it so someday I would be too." Chelsea lowered her head. "I... just want to get along with her. I want us to be happy, together, as a *family*. I'm not sure what I've done wrong, but she *doesn't* like me."

"She's been through a lot. She doesn't understand how much I love you. She likely never will. Don't worry about her. Don't worry about *either* of my parents. I think it's time that you and I spend quality time together here at the cabin. Just you and me. We can focus on building our own family out here." Henry shook his head. "I've been so focused on making the past right but didn't realize I should focus on the future, with you, and our children. I'll take *care* of my parents."

Chelsea managed a thin smile. "I'd like that," she lied. She knew what he meant and hoped it wouldn't come to that. "Now," she said tugging on his hand, "stop wasting time. I have to show you."

Henry kissed her lips. "Okay," he said. "I can't wait."

Chelsea brought him to the shed and demanded he close his eyes before stepping inside. Henry obeyed, covering his face. He took a few steps inside, stumbling with his eyes closed, before looking at her painting, on the floor.

The splashes of paint across the canvas bewildered him. It wasn't what she typically painted. He raised an eyebrow.

Chelsea let out an audible sigh from behind him. "It fell! It's ruined. Some of the paint has run."

Henry looked back at her. "You can barely tell."

Chelsea looked at him, her mouth gaping. "You *don't* like it?"

Henry's eyes widened. "I love it. It's *new* for you. I thought you didn't do abstract paintings."

"I don't, but I wanted to try something new. It fell off the easel, though. It's *ruined!*"

Henry shook his head. "It's great, really. I'll put it on the wall as soon as it dries." Henry stepped into the shed, bending down to pick up her art. When his hand gripped the side of the canvas, there was a snapping sound, and the metal teeth of the large trap shot closed onto Henry's arm.

Henry shouted out in pain. Chelsea quickly shifted some paint cans and grabbed the large kitchen knife she'd concealed earlier.

CHAPTER THIRTY-SEVEN

Martha stepped into the shed and tossed Chelsea to the side. Her body thudded against the wall and she dropped the knife. When Chelsea stood, Martha moved in front of her and shoved her hard. Chelsea tumbled out of the shed, tripping into the dirt.

Martha ran out, jumped on top of her waist and raised a fist. 'I knew you were no good from the moment I met you!" She struck Chelsea in the face, hard. Blood spurted from her nose and Chelsea covered her face with one hand and pleaded for her to stop with the other.

Martha sat on top of her as Chelsea struggled. She looked up and saw Arthur limping towards her from the cabin.

"Grab the gun!" Martha yelled to him. "The tin box is in my dresser. Bring it to me. I have the key on me!" She looked down at Chelsea and smiled. "Looks like I have another hole to dig." Henry screamed inside the shed, thrashing about, kicking against the aluminum side. "You're going to pay for what you did to him!" she snarled at Chelsea.

"Rachel!" Henry yelled. "It hurts! Help me! It hurts." He continued to kick the shed in pain, screaming louder.

Martha turned to her lover. "I'll—" Before she finished, Chelsea struck the bruised side of her face, and she fell off of Chelsea.

Chelsea quickly rolled on top of her and began dropping

her fist hard into Martha's face. Martha screamed as Chelsea continued to strike her and she wasn't able to block her blows. After a relentless flurry of blows, Martha stopped moving.

Henry screamed inside the shed, screaming for someone named Rachel, in between his shrieks of pain.

Chelsea slowly stood up, wiping the blood from her nose.

Arthur was getting closer and looked down at Martha. He took his time getting down on one knee, taking her pulse. "She's not dead."

Chelsea felt a sigh of relief when he said the words. Martha turned to Chelsea, her face battered, and mumbled something.

"I can't hear you, Martha," Chelsea whispered. She looked at Arthur. "I saw some rope in the barn. I'll be right back. Yell if she starts to get up."

Arthur raised his crutch above his head at Martha. "She's not going anywhere."

Chelsea ran quickly into the barn and grabbed the bundle of ropes lying near the wall. She quickly came back and tied Martha's feet together. Then her hands. Martha didn't move. Chelsea put her face against her mouth and felt a warm breath against her cheek.

"I hate you," Martha muttered. "I *hate you*."

Chelsea stood up and looked down at her. "I don't *hate you*. You're one of us," she said. "Who are you, really?"

Martha smiled as Henry called out for Rachel again. "I'm *Rachel*. Henry," she said between heavy breaths, "loves me, *not you*."

Inside the shed, Henry continued to scream in pain. Chelsea looked down at Martha with empathy. "You can have him."

Martha spit out blood.

Chelsea bent down and reached into Martha's neckline, ripping the key chain from her neck. Martha screamed in pain.

"Do you think you can watch them both while I run to the cabin to get the gun?" she asked Arthur.

"That I can manage," Arthur said, looking at Martha with a frown, as Henry shrieked.

Chelsea quickly went to Martha's bedroom and shifted through her dresser. She found an envelope inside and took it out. Inside was a picture of Chelsea. She recognized the scenery immediately. It was the hospital she was at after her father caught her cutting the first time. It was soon after this that she had met Henry. The shot was her candidly walking down the street. She was sure she hadn't met Henry yet at this time.

How long had he been watching me? Chelsea thought. She stuffed the envelope back in the dresser and found the tin box. She opened it with Martha's key and smiled when she saw the handgun.

Chelsea ran back to Arthur as fast as she could. She immediately let out a sigh of relief when she saw Arthur standing over top of Martha and heard Henry in the shed pleading.

"Help me with Henry," she said to Arthur, and he nodded.

Chelsea stepped into the shed. Henry lifted his one good hand, the large kitchen knife Chelsea firmly in his grasp. He laughed. "Come on! *Come on!*"

Chelsea raised the gun and pointed it at him. "Drop it, Henry, or *whoever* you are."

Arthur shook his head. "He brought a knife to a gun fight. It's over, Henry."

Chelsea tilted her head. "Toss the knife."

Henry laughed, wincing in pain as he did. "Or *what*?"

Chelsea looked at Arthur. "Cover your ears." Arthur listened. Chelsea pointed the gun at Henry's leg.

When Henry saw the look in her eye he pleaded. "*Wait!*"

Chelsea pulled the trigger. When nothing happened, she pulled the trigger again.

Arthur smiled. "*Safety's* on, Sea."

Before Chelsea could take it off, Henry tossed the knife to the side of the shed. Chelsea dropped the remaining rope at Henry's feet and gave the gun to Arthur.

"If he tries anything, kill him," she said.

Arthur pointed the gun at Henry's chest. "My pleasure."

Chelsea carefully lowered herself to Henry, wrapping the rope around his feet. When she was finished, she looked up at him.

"Lower your hand," she demanded. "And don't try anything."

Arthur put his finger on the trigger. Henry lowered his head, and his good arm. Chelsea tied his hand to the knot she'd made at his feet.

Chelsea stood up and looked down at Henry. His feet and hand were tied together well.

"Girl Guides?" Arthur asked.

"Girl Guides," Chelsea repeated with a smirk. "Can you give us a moment, Arthur?"

Arthur nodded. "Of course." He handed her the gun. "Get your *closure*." Arthur limped out of the shed.

Chelsea bent down, grabbed the knife and slid it into her belt. She looked back at Henry as he whimpered on the ground.

"What have you done?" he asked her. "We would have had a *great* life together."

"It was all *fake*," Chelsea said. "All of it." She raised the gun at him. "You never loved me!"

"I did!" Henry shouted back.

Chelsea shook her head, seeing Henry for the first time. "You stalked me when I was staying at the psych ward. How long were you watching me?"

"I loved you from the moment I saw you," Henry said, a tear coming down his face. "I wanted us to have the *perfect life*. The perfect family *together*. I knew we could. I just had to make you see the potential we had."

Chelsea shook her head again. "You saw how *vulnerable* I was. You used me." Chelsea looked outside the shed and saw Martha wiggling in the dirt. Chelsea knew she'd tied those ropes tight. She wouldn't be going anywhere. Chelsea looked beyond Martha, into the garden.

She turned and pointed the gun at Henry's head. "You used all of them. Me, Carrie. Arthur, Martha, and whoever else you buried in the garden." Chelsea's mouth tightened. "You *killed* Neil."

"He was the one who wanted to *use* you!" Henry yelled.

Chelsea looked down at Henry, lowering the gun. "I'm not going to kill you, or Martha. I'm not going to bury you in the garden like you would have done to me."

"You were always too good to do what is needed. That's why you *need* me!"

Chelsea clicked the safety on the gun. "I'm not a psycho. You're going to pay for every life you buried in that field. You can't *choose* your family, Henry. You can't pretend to have the perfect family. No family is perfect. I can, though, choose not to be with you." Chelsea laughed. "I want a *fucking* divorce."

Chelsea turned and left him in the shed. As she walked outside, he yelled to her. "Sea! You need me! You need *me*!" Chelsea ignored him. She walked past Martha, who continued to move around on the floor, her arms and legs bound together. She ignored her as well.

She walked up to Arthur. "Are you ready to leave, Arthur?"

He smiled. "I am, but don't call me *Arthur* anymore."

CHAPTER THIRTY-EIGHT

After gathering supplies, Fred and Chelsea made their way through the woods. This time, Chelsea would head towards the truck parked in the lot. Although it would still have flat tires, they would follow the road up to the highway. They had been walking for over an hour but hadn't made it too far from the cabin.

Fred leaned against a tree, catching his breath. "This isn't going to work," he said. "I can't hike this."

"I'm not leaving you," Chelsea said. "I'm not doing that *again*."

Fred took a deep breath. "You're not leaving me. I'm asking you to go. Don't make me beg. If we go together, it will take days before we ever hit the highway. You go on by yourself. Make it to the highway. Get help. I know you'll be back for me. I won't stop. I'll keep moving. Come back and find me, okay?"

Chelsea looked at him, trying to think of something to say to change his mind. "Fine," she admitted, "but you're taking this." She pulled the gun from her waistband.

Arthur shook his head. "I'll take the knife. You're the best shot we have at getting out of here. You need the gun more than me. Just don't forget to take the safety off if you need it." He smirked at her.

Chelsea smiled. "You're much more stubborn than I thought."

"That's what my real wife would always tell me," he said.

"You're *actually* married?"

"Widowed." Fred pushed off the tree. "We will have plenty of time to get to know each other if we can get the hell out of here. So, you go! I'll be fine."

Chelsea nodded and gave him the knife. "I'll be back for you."

Fred smiled back at her. "I know you will, Sea. Now, be careful."

Chelsea left him, taking a moment to get her bearings, and headed in the direction she believed the parking lot was. She would at times run, or jog, and walk. After several hours, she spotted a broken fence line.

Her heart soared, knowing it was the parking lot. From a distance, she spotted Henry's truck. She took out a brownie that her and Henry had bought from the gas station from the backpack and a bottle of water. She started to eat and drink as she got closer to the truck. All she had to do was follow the road and it would lead to the highway.

She stopped walking when she heard a growl behind her. She saw the wolf, and it stared back at her, its teeth showing. Chelsea took the gun out of the backpack and took off the safety. She raised the gun, dropping the water and brownie.

"Leave me alone!" she shouted at the beast. *"Leave me alone!"* She backed away slowly, keeping the gun pointed at it. "I hate you!" she shouted at it. *"I hate you!"*

The wolf got closer, as Chelsea slowly backed away. Chelsea continued to yell at the wolf until it stopped. It lowered its head, gobbling the brownie she'd left behind.

Chelsea laughed to herself, grabbing a few more snacks from the backpack and tossing them towards the wolf. The wolf raised its head at Chelsea, then immediately went back to snacking on its food.

Chelsea continued to walk towards the parking lot, looking back often at the wolf, who was no longer following her. Chelsea walked down the dirt road knowing it would lead to the highway.

After another few hours, she spotted it. When she finally stepped onto the highway, she lowered her head and put it on the cold concrete, laughing.

When she raised her head, she saw two boys playing in the ditch beside the highway, looking at her. She immediately recognized them as the boys she'd seen at the gas station in the town nearby.

"You!" she shouted at the kids. The boys immediately climbed out of the ditch and hurried to their bikes, but Chelsea ran ahead of them and grabbed the handlebar of one. "I need your phone!" she demanded of them.

"We don't have one right now," the boy who'd tried to steal her phone a few days ago explained.

"*Bull!*' she shouted. "I'm not joking, I need to call the police!"

"He's telling the truth, miss!" the other boy shouted. "We're not lying."

Chelsea sighed. "I need the nearest phone, now! Where would it be?"

The boy in the red shirt pointed down the road. "The gas station, where we met you before. It's about an hour's ride."

Chelsea took a bottle of water from her backpack, downing it, some of it leaking down her hand onto her shirt.

She pulled the bike away from the boy. "Your bike will be at the gas station." Chelsea sat on the saddle and turned away. She started to peddle as the boy yelled out to her.

"Stop! You stole my bike!"

Chelsea peddled as fast as she could. Any time she slowed, she thought of Fred in the woods by himself. She didn't know what time it was, but it felt it was mid-afternoonish. She needed to get help and go back to Fred as soon as she could.

When she saw the lonesome gas station, she nearly cried. She maintained her composure and rolled the bicycle next to the door. She got off the bike and let it drop to the cement floor. She threw open the gas station door.

The gas station attendant sat behind the counter reading a paper, not caring about her presence in his store. "Pump is unlocked," he said to her. "When you're done pumping, come back inside and pay."

"I need your phone to call the police," Chelsea said between breaths.

The attendant lowered the paper and gave her an awkward stare. He looked even more like an asshole then she remembered. "*Why*?" he asked in a nasty tone.

Chelsea didn't answer. Instead, she walked behind his counter, grabbed the cordless phone, and walked towards the exit.

"Hey!" the man yelled at her, but she ignored him.

She dialed 911 and waited for a voice.

"911, what's your emergency?" a woman asked.

Chelsea stood in front of the bulletin board in the gas bar. On it were all the missing people she had seen before. One of the names immediately caught her attention.

Caroline Sanders. She recognized the picture of Henry's ex now. Below her name on the poster, it read that she also goes by "Carrie".

Chelsea cleared her throat into the phone. "I need help."

CHAPTER THIRTY-NINE

It took several hours for Chelsea to explain what had happened at the cabin. When she told them that Caroline Sanders' body was buried there, they began listening better. A large search party was formed by mostly police, including a canine unit, and paramedics.

Chelsea demanded that she led the detectives to the cabin herself. A paramedic had medically cleared her to go and the detective in charge agreed.

A caravan of police vehicles and ambulances made its way down Highway One. Eventually, they passed the hamlet where the gas station was located, and Chelsea guided them to where Henry had parked his truck.

The vehicles surrounded Henry's in the nearly empty lot. His truck was searched immediately but nothing out of the ordinary was found inside.

The head detective, Mr. Aldridge, was an older man, who came off indifferent to the terrible things he had seen on the job. He looked mean, except when talking to Chelsea, when his face lightened at her words. Despite his bulletproof demeanour, Chelsea knew he must have been through a lot in his time in policing.

When Detective Aldridge cleared her to exit the patrol vehicle she did, and she pointed in the general direction of the cabin. "It's this way." She took in a deep breath, looking around the pitch dark woods. "What time is it now?"

Aldridge looked at his watch. "Almost ten."

Chelsea panicked inside. She had left Fred in the woods for the entire day. She thought of the wolf. She had told Aldridge about the lingering animal ahead of time. He didn't expect much trouble with the amount of manpower and dogs they had in their entourage.

"Let's get the lights on, boys!" Aldridge yelled. Within a few minutes, the entire forest was illuminated like it was daytime.

"It's this way!' Chelsea yelled. She led the group along the path she remembered taking with Henry only a few days before. She looked at Alridge. "Four-hour hike to the cabin from here."

Detective Alridge smiled back. "I believe it. This is a provincial park. There was a broken-down sign that said so. How the hell could someone be living out here and nobody knew?"

They group trekked through the woods, illuminating every inch of darkness as they did. Dogs barked. Members of the group used whistles.

Several hours into the woods, Chelsea was starting to panic. They hadn't found Fred yet. She was sure he would have made it further into the woods by now. He could have gotten lost when trying to find the parking lot.

Every so often Chelsea would yell out his name, hoping to hear his voice in the darkness. All she heard was other group members and their dogs.

She pictured the bright light uncovering his body laying on the ground, dead. She tried not to think about that and continued to search the lit areas for him.

Suddenly a dark figure waved and called out. "Here!"

Chelsea ran to it.

"Mrs. Jameson," Detective Aldridge yelled, but she didn't stop.

She ran past the police lights, until she reached him.

Fred smiled back at her in the darkness. "I thought you didn't make it."

Chelsea held his hands. "A few times I didn't think I would either. Are you any worse?"

Fred shook his head. "No. Same. Feeling like *shit*. I couldn't walk much further."

"Don't worry." Chelsea turned her head and yelled at her group. "I need a paramedic here!"

The paramedics immediately placed Fred on a stretcher and picked him up. Several held him in place as they walked back towards the parking lot. A police officer followed.

Chelsea waved to Fred. "We did it!"

He waved back. "No, *you* did it. I owe you my life! Come see me after!"

Chelsea knew Fred had tried to save her more than once himself, but took his compliment. "I will! Get better!" Chelsea looked for Detective Aldridge. "We should be at the cabin within the hour or so."

Soon the police lights caught the barn in the darkness. Chelsea pointed it out to Aldridge. "I tied up Martha right outside the shed, near the barn! Henry is inside the shed too!"

Chelsea again ran ahead of the group. She needed to know Martha and Henry were still there. Detective Aldridge kept pace, drawing his revolver and holding it at his side.

"Slow down, Mrs. Jameson," he said to her.

Chelsea shook her head. "Don't call me by that name."

She was near the shed, but didn't see Martha. She peered around in the darkness, only the moonlight illuminating her view. Detective Aldridge took out his flashlight and looked at her.

"She could have wiggled her way into the barn," Chelsea said, breathing heavily.

"I'm afraid not," Detective Aldridge said, bending down. When he stood up, he handed her the thick ropes. "They look like they've been cut."

Chelsea knew immediately what had happened. Martha's knife. She had it on her when Chelsea tied her. How could she have forgotten?

Martha had waited for her to leave before she escaped, *with him.*

Chelsea ran to the shed, but slowly stepped inside. Part of her was worried Martha and Henry were waiting for her in the darkness until she turned on the inside light and covered her mouth.

Henry's head was slumped to one side. His white shirt had multiple rips, red stains coming from each one. In the center of his chest was a small Swiss army knife with a pink heart on it.

CHAPTER FORTY

One year later.

Chelsea continued to set up her wall at the gala. There were still a few hours left before the students of the art program at the University of Toronto would unveil their artwork to anybody interested to see it. It was mostly family members who would be there, she was told. Chelsea knew that with her having no family left, she might not get too many guests to her wall. Still, she had a speech ready. You never knew who would show up.

She had had more than *fifteen minutes of fame* after what happened at the cabin. Multiple documentaries had been made. Another film crew had interviewed her the week before to give a one-year update on how she was doing today. A biographer wanted to work with her on her life story. He claimed they already had a television studio interested in the rights for a TV movie.

Chelsea refused, though. It was time for her to move on in life.

She lifted a large canvas and hung it on the display wall. She already had more than double the paintings of any other student. She had so many ideas, and not enough hands to paint them all at once. Only a few made it to the wall for the gala, though.

Another artist named Theresa was on the wall beside her. Her artwork involved a lot of mirrors in her pieces. She'd named her wall "Reflection" in bright mirrored letters. Theresa struggled with a larger mirror, nearly dropping it. Chelsea ran to her and picked up the other side.

"Thanks!" Theresa said. She motioned to where it would be hung, and Chelsea helped.

After the large, mirrored art was on the wall, Chelsea took a moment to regard herself. She looked slender in her sleeveless red dress. Her bare arms were something she was still getting used to. Sometimes people would notice the cuts, but Chelsea no longer cared.

She smiled at her image in the mirror. Her smile grew when she saw a man limping behind her.

"You look great, Sea," Fred said.

Chelsea hugged him tightly. "I didn't think you would travel all this way!"

"Wouldn't miss it," he said. A little girl ran up to him and hugged his legs. "This is Debbie!" he said, bending over to pick her up. "My granddaughter, she's seven now." He had missed years with his grandchild when he was at the cabin, but with the smile on his face you wouldn't know it.

Behind Fred, a younger woman waved at them.

"My daughter, Eve," Fred said. "Eve, well, this is my other *daughter*, Chelsea."

Eve walked up to them, tickling her daughter, who giggled. "I want to thank you," she said to Chelsea. "I didn't think... well, he's back." She smiled. "*Thank you.*"

"He saved me more than once too," Chelsea said with a smirk.

Fred laughed. "Listen, we want to take you to dinner after the gala. Would that be okay? We're in the city for a few days, too."

"I am definitely free," Chelsea said.

"Look at all of these!" Eve said, staring at her paintings. "These are beautiful."

"Can I have one, Momma?" the little girl, Debbie, asked.

"These are great," Fred said. "I know I've seen one of these before though." He pointed at the abstract painting she'd made for Henry, hung prominently in the middle of her wall.

"Not my *favourite* one," Chelsea said. "Sometimes you're not always happy about the past, though." She looked down at her wrists and back at Fred. "But you need to forgive yourself, because that's a part of you. It's actually the theme of my wall."

Fred smiled. "I like that. Are you ready to show everyone your paintings?"

"I feel like you guys are it for me tonight. I don't think too many people will care besides you."

Eve laughed. "I saw a few camera crews outside. One of them mentioned your name. I don't think so. I think you're going to have some attention today."

Chelsea shook her head. "Ah, hell."

"What?" Fred asked. "What's wrong?"

"This speech I'm going to give for my paintings. I hate speeches. I was truly hoping it would only be you guys."

"Well," Fred said, "practice the speech on us." Chelsea laughed but Fred folded his arms, waiting. "Go ahead. You can mess up in front of us if you want."

Chelsea smiled. Somehow, she knew Fred was just as stubborn a man she had met in the cabin when she called him Arthur. "Fine." Chelsea walked in front of her wall and turned to her small crowd. "Ladies and gentlemen. *Changes.* All of us change throughout life. Some change is for the better, and sometimes not. These paintings reflect some of my changes." Chelsea pointed towards an empty area. "Pretend there's a painting here. A real good painting. I'm still getting ready." Chelsea cleared her throat. "This painting reflects my change for the future. It's full of promise. I take with me all my baggage from the past. It's up to me what I do with the lessons I've learned."

Chelsea pointed at a picture of a little girl with a microphone, her hands raised, standing on top of the head of a giant. The giant had long flowing hair that matched the little girl's. "Finding your voice can be hard, but if you love yourself, and all your flaws—" Chelsea looked down at her bare arm a moment, smiling to herself. "—then it becomes easier." Chelsea moved down the wall and pointed at a picture of young woman wearing a sundress, leaning against a skull. "Along the way to finding yourself, and loving yourself, you will reflect on the people in your *circle*. Sometimes you may feel certain people are the only reasons your life is good. You can become co-dependent on others for your own happiness, and when that happens, hopefully those people have good intentions for you. It's okay to lean on others when you need help." Chelsea looked at Fred and smiled. "You need to stand on your own as well." Chelsea went back to the abstract picture she'd painted at the cabin last. She looked at it, remembering all the emotion she had when she painted it. "It's important to remember, though, that no matter where you are in life, you're not trapped. You can *change*."

CHAPTER FORTY-ONE

Adam Kilbourn sat at the table in the restaurant, waiting for his date to return from the bathroom. He couldn't remember the last time he'd had such a fun time with a woman since his wife passed. He couldn't remember the last time he'd had a date for that matter.

It had been years since his wife left this earth, and he felt he still had more love to give. Dating in your sixties wasn't an easy thing to do, though. Things had changed from when he was a young single boy prowling for women.

Dating apps. Tinder. None of these things made sense to him. Hooking up seemed to be the new norm in the dating world, but all Adam wanted was a good woman to lay with. Talk for hours. Enjoy each other's company.

It was surprising to Adam that he'd been able to meet someone through a local newspaper that promised to match couples who were older on blind dates.

His date was beautiful. With her flowy sundress, she had a youthful appearance. She said she was in her fifties but didn't look a day over forty.

Their conversation had been going well. They had many things in common already. A sad one was the fact that she was widowed too after many years of being with her husband.

The waiter walked by the table and asked if he wanted more wine, but Adam shook his head. He didn't want to mess up tonight. She seemed to find him charming. More wine wouldn't help with that.

Finally, she came back to the table with a smile that

matched Adam's.

"Hope I didn't keep you long," she said.

"I would have waited for you." Adam said. He knew it was corny, but his wife had always loved his corny flirts.

"You're too good," she said with a smile.

Adam cleared his throat and leaned forward. "So, Rachel, what are you looking for right now?"

Rachel smiled. "You don't beat around the bush, do you?"

"Not at my *tender* age."

Rachel sipped her wine. "I'm looking for *love*. For someone to love me. I want a *family*."

"Family?" Adam asked with a smile.

Rachel smiled. "Oh yes. I know we're at a tender age, but it's never too late to choose your *family*."

Note from the author:

I truly hope you enjoyed reading my story as much as I did creating it. As an indie author, what you think of my book is all I care about.

If you enjoyed my story, please take a moment to leave your review on the Amazon store. It would mean the world to me.

Thank you for reading, and I hope you join me next time.

Download My Free Book

A PSYCHOLOGICAL THRILLER

THE
AFFAIR

JAMES CAINE

If you would like to receive a FREE
copy of my psychological thriller, The Affair,
then please click the button below.

Alice Ruffalo is on the run from her violent husband. She believes she found safety in a rundown motel in a small town.

The handsome motel clerk helps take her mind off her fears, until she starts to hear weird sounds outside her motel room and sees shadowy figures near her door.

Alice finds out the hard way that she shouldn't have stopped in this small town. Her husband knows exactly where she is.

★★★★★ *"This is such a thrilling read." Goodreads reviewer*

★★★★★ "A brilliant read. " Goodreads reviewer

**Please email me at
jamescaineauthor@gmail.com if you
would like the link to my free story.**

Thanks again,

James

THE PATIENT'S LIST

The new patient whispered a list of names. One by one they're each dying.

Rina Kent was the new hot shot psychiatrist at Holy Saints ward. She also recently married the love of her life, who's also a doctor at the same hospital. Rina felt on top of the world, until one of her patients committed suicide.

Rina knows it was **her fault.**

A year later, her marriage has already gone down in flames. All she has left is her patients, but she's lost her confidence to help them.

When a suicidal teenaged girl comes to her ward, Rina sees a second chance to help the patient she couldn't save. The new girl won't say a word to anyone though and Rina's colleagues already feel she's a lost cause.

She begins to wonder if her peers are right, when one night the girl shyly walks up to Rina and whispers a list of names.

What Rina can't understand is why the last name she says is her ex-husband's.

James Caine, the author of The In-Laws, and The Girl Outside, offers another psychological thriller novel with many twists and turns that you will not know what to believe or who to trust.

Please enjoy this sneak preview of The Patient's List:

Prologue

Amy, always know that your mother loves you. I will do anything to make sure you have a better life than I had. I will do anything to protect you.

No matter what happens, always know that everything I do, I do for you.

No matter what happens, never say a word.

Chapter 1

Rina Kent smiled as her handsome husband walked down the stairs to greet her in the kitchen. They were already running late for their shift at the hospital, but Rina made him a grand breakfast. Being newly married, she knew the giddy feelings for Jonas would lessen over time, at least that's what she heard from her married friends. She would try not to worry about the eventual lows they would have and focus on how happy she was in the moment.

"Good morning, Dr. Kent," Jonas said playfully, coming up behind her, firmly squeezing her rear, and kissing her neck. Rina sighed. If they weren't running late, she would try and get more of what she had this morning.

She turned and kissed her husband. "Good morning, Dr. Kent." Her smile grew and they kissed again.

"Whatever you're whipping up smells amazing," Jonas said. "We need to scarf it down though. We're—"

"Going to be late, I know. I couldn't help myself."

Rina took off a few pieces of sizzling bacon and added it to the container. Denzel, their brown miniature poodle puppy, rubbed up against Rina's ankle, barking. Denzel, whose last name would be Washington if he required one, was the first gift Jonas surprised Rina with after they moved in together. For their wedding they trained him to walk down the aisle with the wedding bands.   Thankfully they trained him well.

Jonas grabbed a piece of bacon from the covered bowl and ripped off half, giving it to him. "We should take separate cars today. I think I'll be done at the ER a little later than you. Try not to stay too late on the ward. The flight is in ten hours. We need to be at the airport at least three hours before."

Rina laughed. "Three hours! That's way too long to be at the airport. Don't worry," she said, palming her husband's face, "we won't miss the flight to our honeymoon."

"Two weeks in Aruba," he said with a devilish smile. "The first twenty-four hours, I want you to wear nothing. Promise?"

Rina kissed him again, taking her time to feel his soft lips. "An easy one to keep."

Jonas bent down and patted Denzel. "Sorry, boy, you're not coming." Denzel didn't appear to care, nearly smiling while being pet.

They ate their breakfast quickly. Rina brought some of it to her car and ate on the road. Luckily, they only lived ten minutes away from the hospital. Still, somehow, she found herself nearly late for her shift often.

She parked her car in the Holy Saints staff lot. She rolled her eyes when she noticed that Jonas was already parked in his designated spot for ER doctors neat the entrance. Even though he left after she did, he always seemed to find a way to get where they were going before her.

A nurse walked towards her vehicle and waved. Rina smiled and waved back to her. She felt terrible, forgetting her name.

Vanessa, she thought. Or was it Valorie? Whatever her name was, she had seen her in the halls at the hospital, turning a few of her male colleagues' heads as she walked by. A blond bombshell, Rina believed was the term.

Rina was pretty, she knew, but sometimes when she observed the beauty of those a little younger, a little fitter than her, it somehow made her feel insecure. It could be that she turned thirty last month, and she knew her body would continue to change, be less... beautiful.

Rina looked at her watch and started to quicken her pace. She entered the four-storey hospital and made her way quickly past the greeting staff to the elevators.

She grimaced when she saw that they were out of order, again. How many times had Rina needed to take the stairs in this old building? She looked back towards the visitor's information desk. Displayed proudly was a sign showing that the construction of the new hospital had started, and someday in the near future, Holy Saints would be demolished. Rina might clap when that day came. She had only been working as a psychiatrist for a few years, and only one of those at Holy Saints. The building was past its prime decades ago.

Once she'd made her way up the stairs to the fourth floor, she inhaled deeply, trying to catch her breath before opening the door.

When Rina entered her floor, she waved at the new security guard, Ryan. Ryan was a tall young man, with a stubble beard. The truth was that she didn't much like him. She had caught him more than once sleeping in his office when she popped in to ask a security question regarding a patient. Night shifts were brutal, Rina knew, but sleeping on the job when he was sometimes the only person that could catch a patient sneaking off the psych ward made her pissed beyond belief. What would happen if someone got away? Patients' safety on her ward was extremely important for Rina.

Most of the time Rina would only greet him good morning or good night but today he smiled at her.

"Congratulations!" he said.

"Thanks, Ryan," Rina said. He waved his security pass at the door system, and the red light above the psych ward door turned green, then back to red instantly. "Door's having problems again?"

"Nothing works at this hospital," Ryan scoffed. He waved his pass again and the light above turned green and stayed that way, allowing Rina to enter her ward.

She'd only managed to take a few steps before a patient of hers came up to her. "Dr. Thennley," she said shyly.

"Morning, Jenny," Rina said with a soft smile. "It's Dr. Kent now, though. I'm sure it will be hard for many, especially me, to get used to that."

Jenny lowered her head. "I had a bit of a hard weekend. Can we talk?"

"I'm sorry to hear, Jenny. Let's talk. Can I get settled in first, though? I'll come right back and find you. Okay?"

Jenny nodded. "Okay."

Rina thanked her and headed towards the main rec area. Patients were lined up taking their medicine from Nurse Bethany Myder. Already she could hear the coarse voice of the nurse demanding some of the patients who didn't require morning meds to step out of the line.

Sometimes Rina thought of Bethany as the sheriff of the ward, instead of a psychiatric nurse. She had voiced her concerns to the Chief of Psychiatry, Dr. Greber, but he said he wasn't able to do much about her. Her union protected her, even though she had managed to give the wrong medications to several patients in the past six months, in addition to her abusive tone with the patients.

Rina looked past her to the large windows. She always enjoyed taking in the view from the rec room that faced the dense woods beyond the parking lot. She enjoyed bird watching from here with some patients. It was a calming activity, looking out into forest.

Nurse Bethany barked at a patient, "Stop it, Edward. You

know I need to see you take the pills! Now, open your mouth." The patient was new to the ward this week. He had been sectioned by police after attacking his neighbor for thinking he was an alien. Schizophrenia was such a difficult diagnosis to work with at first and required a lot of building trust with a patient for better results.

"Good morning, Edward," Rina said, interjecting. "How are you?"

Edward smiled. "Morning, Dr. The— or Dr. Kent, now, right?"

"Great memory, Ed. Is everything okay with your new meds?"

"I was just making sure he took his pills, Dr. Kent," Nurse Bethany said sternly.

"Thanks, Bethany." Rina didn't look at her. If she had, she wouldn't have been able to hide her disgust for the woman at that moment. "Are you having any bad side effects?"

"I haven't been sleeping," Ed said, rubbing the side of his head. "The meds are making it impossible."

Rina nodded. "Let's chat really quick before I leave. I can lessen the dose. Figuring out the best medications can be difficult but once we do you will feel so much better."

"Thanks, Doc," Ed said. "Do I need to take these, then?"

"How about you give those back to Bethany, and when we meet in my office, we can fix your meds?"

Ed thanked her again and went across the rec room to grab a puzzle from the shelf. Rina noticed her colleagues, Dr. Sarah Alloy and Dr. Adam Greber, talking to each other. Dr. Greber was in his last month as the chief psychiatrist at Holy Saints hospital.

It was said that either Rina or Dr. Alloy would be up for the promotion after Dr. Greber retired. The only fault Rina thought she had was her tardiness. If she were to self-evaluate she thought she was better at connecting with patients, building strong rapports with them that helped with their recovery. Dr. Alloy had been a psychiatrist at Holy Saints for over five years. She had been biding her time for this promotion.

Even though Rina had only been on staff for the past year, she knew she had the edge on her colleague. She could only imagine the frustration Sarah felt.

"Next!" Nurse Bethany called, and another patient came up to her.

Rina looked at a small foldable table that had some pamphlets on it. She shook her head. It was the only furniture in the room not stuck to the ground, which wasn't protocol.

"We should probably put these pamphlets somewhere else," she said to Bethany.

"Talk to Dr. Alloy," Bethany barked back. "She put the table here. It's not my job to move it."

Rina sighed. She picked up a pamphlet. It was about a new outpatient program that Sarah was running for patients after they were discharged. The printed sheet had only Dr. Alloy's name on it, not Rina's even though it was Rina's idea to have stronger outpatient support. She had brought it up in conversation with Sarah about a week ago, and her colleague had disregarded it, suggesting their caseloads were already heavy enough and there was no financing for additional staff.

Rina looked back at Sarah Alloy talking to the soon to be retired Dr. Greber. It was obvious what Sarah was doing. She wanted to show her initiative. Sure, it annoyed her that Sarah would put only her name on the program's information, but what made Rina really upset was the table itself. There was a reason why no furniture could be movable, and everything was secured to the floor. It was for the patients' safety.

Part of Rina wanted to interrupt their conversation to tell Sarah about the safety hazard she made in the ward in front of Dr. Greber. Rina reminded herself that she was leaving on her honeymoon today. She didn't want bad blood between her and Sarah. After all, no matter who got the promotion, they would still be working with each other. She would be sure to tell Sarah about her concerns in private.

In her peripheral vision she spotted Jenny Berange, her head down, in the corner of the room. Rina had seen her this way before when she was first admitted to Holy Saints. She had been brought to the ward after police talked her down from jumping off a bridge into the Bow River. The first few days at the unit, Jenny would stand in the corner beside the window for hours at a time, not wanting to talk to anyone.

Rina had worked tirelessly on finding a connection with her. She was only nineteen. A pretty young girl, with so much potential ahead of her if she could get her mental health in line. Being her assigned psychiatrist, Rina had read her file, of course. She knew the abuse she took from her father. She knew the neglect her mother had for her. She had been diagnosed with acute psychosis and feared that unknown forces were after her.

When no progress was being made with Jenny, many had assumed she would be discharged and attempt to kill herself again. Rina had continued to work on finding a connection with the young woman. One morning she observed that Jenny was reading an Agatha Christie novel while standing in the corner. Rina brought similar books from her home library for Jenny and would put them on a table near where she stood. Eventually, Jenny started to read them. Then Rina would spend clinical time reading with her and discussing their favourite parts of the stories. It was almost as if they had started a book club for the two of them. Within a week she was a different person to the distraught girl escorted to the ward.

Now, Rina looked at Jenny standing in the corner of the room as if it were her first day again at Holy Saints. She took a deep breath. Mental health could be very circular in nature. You get better, then worse. Many people who struggled were never a hundred percent better in the end, but hopefully had more tools for taking better care of themselves by the time they left the ward. Whenever her patients were at a low point, all Rina could do was help them with medicine and techniques for handling their symptoms.

Rina was about to ask Jenny to chat in her office when she saw Sarah and Dr. Greber walk towards her, and she put the pamphlet back down on the table.

"Morning, Dr. Kent," Dr Greber said. "That was a fun wedding.

I'm surprised we don't have too many hungover doctors and nurses around this morning."

Rina laughed. "Well, they had Sunday to recover."

"Congratulations, Rina," Sarah said. "So, you're only working a little today, right? When's your flight?"

Rina was annoyed at the mention of her reduced hours so she could leave on her honeymoon but smiled. "In seven hours."

Dr. Greber interjected. "We need to have a quick meeting."

"No problem," Rina said.

The three of them walked down the hall to Dr. Greber's office. He shut the door behind him. "We should do our roundtable review of our patients before you leave."

Rina sometimes hated these reviews. It was important for them to discuss patients and their recoveries. Dr. Greber would add his input when needed, but mostly let Sarah and Rina do what they felt was required. He was a good boss in that way, she thought. He didn't micromanage people or their personalities. He trusted his staff and knew when he needed to be involved.

Rina hoped that someday she would be as good of a chief psychiatrist as Adam Greber, if she got the job. Interviews would be starting in a month.

After an hour of reviewing patients, Dr. Greber mentioned Jenny's case.

"Great work with Jenny," he said. "Truly amazing how she opened up to you. It's remarkable how you've developed the rapport you have with her in such a short time. You brought home some of your charts for her case file. I wanted to look at them with a special group I'm a part of where we review rapport development with patients. I was hoping to use Jenny's case as a prime example of how to do it well."

Rina smiled. "Thanks, Adam." She tutted. "I forgot them in the car though. I'll run out right now."

"Those are confidential reports, Rina," Sarah said with a tone. "Try not to forget them in your vehicle."

"It's a simple mistake, Sarah," Adam replied. He looked at Rina. "Please grab them, though."

Rina stood up from the couch and nodded to Sarah before leaving the office. She had to bite her tongue at how annoyed she was at her colleague, who was obviously attempting to make her look bad. Rina immediately went down the hall, passing the rec room again.

Jenny wasn't in the corner. She was by the foldable table, looking at the pamphlet.

Rina walked up to her. "Is that program something you would be interested in, Jenny? It's not just Dr. Alloy doing it, but me too. I would love to see you even after your time in Holy Saints."

Jenny put the pamphlet down, lowering her head.

"Jenny?" Rina asked. "I need to go to the parking lot to grab something. Can you wait by my office? I'll be right there, and we can talk. Please."

Jenny raised her head. "They have no eyes," she said in a whisper, "but they see... They have no ears, but they hear – everything."

Rina took a deep breath. She hadn't heard Jenny talk this way for some time. She knew whatever set her off this weekend would be a big blow to her progress. A change in medications would certainly need to be considered.

"Jenny," she said, touching her shoulder gently, "please wait by my office. I'll be right there."

Jenny took a few steps in that direction. "Okay, Dr. Kent."

Rina watched her patient slowly walk away, feeling saddened for the young girl. She had been talking to a social worker about emergency housing for Jenny. Her parents wanted her to return home with them, but given the details in her file, Rina worried about the environment she would be returning to.

Sarah and Adam left the office down the hall and she snapped out of it. She hurried past Ryan, the security guard, down the stairs and back into the parking lot. She ran to her car and opened the door, looking around the nearly empty vehicle to find only a few Starbucks coffee cups, half drunk, in the cup holders.

She panicked, thinking of the conversation she would

have with Dr. Greber and Sarah. "Oh – I only misplaced Jenny Berange's file. No big deal, right?" Sarah Alloy was already on a roll today, throwing Rina under the bus any time she could to make herself look better.

She tried to think back to what she did with the file after she left work yesterday. She vividly remembered taking the file from her office and leaving the ward with it. She remembered getting into Jonas's car and him making a comment about taking work home with her again.

Of course, she'd left it in Jonas's car. They drove to work together that day since they had the same shift. She locked her car and ran across the parking lot to her husband's car. She peeked through the back passenger window and sitting neatly on the black leather seating was the file.

Now she would have to get the keys from Jonas and get the file at light speed. She could already imagine the things Sarah would be saying to Adam Greber if she didn't promptly return.

"Rina's a fine psychiatrist – but unorganized. You need someone who will be here on time, and ready for her day. When you retire, don't you want someone to carry on your legacy in a decent way?"

She could almost see Sarah's smile as she delivered her speech. Happy that she didn't have to do anything besides let Rina be Rina to get the promotion.

A loud crash above her made Rina look up. Large pieces of glass fell around her. Rina covered her eyes but felt a shard cut her forearm and winced in pain.

Something heavy bounced off Jonas's car, and there was a deep thud on the concrete in front of her.

When she removed her hand from her eyes, the disfigured body of Jenny lay in front of her. Her limbs, now pointing at unnatural angles, convulsed, reaching out.   Within moments, she stopped moving.

Rina turned away and found the table from the rec room had landed on Jonas's car. Pamphlets for Sarah's outpatient program were scattered across the roof and surrounding area. Pieces of glass continued to sprinkle from the fourth-floor window. Rina covered her mouth to muffle her screams.

She stopped as she felt the pain in her arm. Blood was running from the large gash on it.

"Are you okay?" she heard a voice call out, but Rina didn't address them. Instead, she looked one last time at her patient, Jenny.

Chapter 2

Six months later.

Dr. Adam Gerber sat at his dining table, the intruder in his home sitting across from him. He took a sip of the fresh orange juice his wife made that day. As he did, his hand shook uncontrollably, spilling it over his suit jacket.

Adam tried not to look at the intruder's face, even though it was covered with a black ski mask. He especially tried not to look at the intruder's handgun, which was aimed directly at his chest. Adam trembled as he put the cup of juice back on the table and took a bite of his biscuit. There was something calming in doing something normal during something chaotic.

The masked intruder had entered his home right after his wife, Vanessa, left to go to their son's for the day to babysit his grandson. The intruder didn't even have to break in, since the door wasn't locked. Nobody in the small town of Carrington, Alberta, locked their doors. Vanessa was not so trusting. She'd grown up in the larger city of Calgary, where crime was more commonplace. She would remind Adam several times a week to lock the doors, but Adam Greber had never been used to the practise. He tried not to imagine his wife saying, "I told you so, Adam."

"You can... take whatever you want," Adam said, his voice trembling as much as his hands. When the Intruder didn't respond, he lowered his head. "I have... money. I have a lot of money."

"Are you finished?" the intruder asked. Adam looked at them now. The thought of being robbed scared him so he couldn't think straight, but the voice of his intruder knocked him out of his daze. He knew exactly who it was.   The intruder took off their ski mask, confirming their identity.

"Why?" Adam asked. "Why now?"

"You know why," the intruder said with a smile.

"The girl?" Adam answered. "It's about the girl, isn't it?"

This time the intruder didn't verbally respond but raised the gun at Adam's head.

"No!" he pleaded. "Wait! I did nothing wrong! I promised. We promised we wouldn't hurt her! She will be fine!"

"Are you finished with your... snack?" the intruder asked again.

Adam took a quick sip of his wife's juice. "I... I have kids, you know. Grandkids!"

The intruder smiled. "I know, Adam. I know."

Adam put his head down. "What I'm saying is, I wouldn't hurt that girl, because I'm a father myself."

"I think you're finished now," the intruder said, standing from their chair, and raising the gun. "You should have done something better with your retirement than what you did! Now you pay for your sins."

"But!" Adam shouted. "You don't have to—"

He saw the muzzle flash, followed by a push on his chest. He fell backwards, landing on his kitchen floor. He looked up and saw his blood staining his white kitchen backsplash. He turned to his side, screaming. Sliding his body across the tiled floor, leaving a trail of his life's blood like a snail behind him.

The intruder stepped in front of him.

"No!" Adam cried out. He looked up at the intruder one last time. He raised his arm towards them in a plea, but they kicked his hand with their boot.

The intruder smiled. "I know you won't hurt her – now."

Adam heard the click of the intruder's gun, and then nothing at all.

Chapter 3

Rina Kent parked in her usual spot at Holy Saints. She was nearly two hours early. She walked through the lot, noticing Jonas's car in his regular space. She covered her head with her hand in a poor attempt to slow the rain from drenching her. The rainfall had been extreme in the past week to the point that local beaches were closed due to high water and stronger currents. Some areas of Carrington were temporarily closed due to flood damage and the formation of large puddles in the streets.

Rina gazed up at the fourth-floor window of the psych ward, rain striking her face forcefully. Rina hated passing the spot where it happened, but there was no other way for employees to get to the building.

Besides, everything was repaired now. Everything was back to how it was supposed to be. Jonas's car was fixed, as if nothing had happened. The rec room window was replaced. The ward had patients check in and check out, as usual.

Everything around Rina had gone back to normal. Rina looked down at her ringless finger. Everything had gone back to... almost normal.

She quickly made her way into the hospital, and up to the fourth floor. She passed Ryan the security guard without a word.

He opened the door after a few swipes of his pass, admitting her inside.

She walked past the rec room, where Nurse Bethany was already reminding patients that it would be time for them to go to their rooms for the night soon. As always, everything the nurse said reminded her more of an order.

"Lights out soon!" she barked. The patients largely ignored her, resuming their activities as if nothing had been said. Most of them knew the routine without her forceful prompts.

Bethany gave Rina an ugly smile. "Early for your night shift, Dr. Thennley."

Nurse Bethany had been starting to call Rina by her maiden name, even though she hadn't officially changed it. Even though Rina had reminded her that it was still "Dr. Kent", she continued to make the mistake.

"Everything okay tonight?" Rina asked.

Bethany nodded. She rubbed her eyes, smudging some of her dark blue eyeshadow. "All fine. Are you only working nights at the hospital now?"

Rina took a deep breath. The psychiatrists took turns doing the overnight rotations. Lately she had been opting to only work midnights and had requested to Dr. Alloy, now the Chief of Psychiatry, that she do so permanently. She could see no reason why Sarah would deny this to her. Rina still kept hours during the daytime for clinical work with her assigned patients but she was available for the entire hospital during her midnight shifts.

Rina knew firsthand the struggles of shift work. It would be better for the psychiatrists at Holy Saints to have a permanent night psychiatrist. Consistent workdays were a positive change that could benefit everyone. She would ask Sarah for an update on her request soon.

Since she'd been awarded the promotion after Dr. Greber retired the month before, Rina had to admit that her new boss was doing a great job. Things were running smoothly in the ward, and in the hospital. All psychiatric care needs were met.

Midnights were best for Rina. She barely slept through the

night anyway. She had better luck napping in the day. Besides, it was easier to avoid her ex-husband at night. He rarely worked midnights in his rotation. Seeing him less made things... a little easier.

"I'm going for my workout," Rina said, ignoring Bethany's question. "If you need me, you can find me at the gym."

Bethany smiled. "I won't need you. Dr. Alloy and Dr. Knowles are still here."

Dr. Belinda Knowles was recently hired as Holy Saints new psychiatrist on the ward after Sarah was promoted. Rina was surprised to hear that. Typically, Dr. Knowles would switch with Rina between morning and night shifts. Sarah, though, would typically be gone before Rina started.

"Why are they here?" she asked.

Bethany looked over her shoulder towards a conference room. "A new girl was admitted today."

Printed in Great Britain
by Amazon

30873779R00117